INSPIRING LEGENDS AND TALES
WITH A MORAL I

Stories From Around the World

Emerson Klees (signature)

Emerson Klees

The Human Values Series

Cameo Press, Rochester, New York

The Human Values Series

Role Models of Human Values

One Plus One Equals Three—Pairing Man / Woman Strengths:
   Role Models of Teamwork (1998)
Entrepreneurs in History—Success vs. Failure:
   Entrepreneurial Role Models (1999)
Staying With It: Role Models of Perseverance (1999)
The Drive to Succeed: Role Models of Motivation (2002)
The Will to Stay With It: Role Models of Determination (2002)

The Moral Navigator

Inspiring Legends and Tales With a Moral I: Stories From
   Around the World (2007)
Inspiring Legends and Tales With a Moral II: Stories From
   Around the World (2007)
Inspiring Legends and Tales With a Moral III: Stories From
   Around the World (2007)

Copyright © 2007 by Emerson C. Klees

Cameo Press
P. O. Box 18131
Rochester, New York 14618

Library of Congress Control Number: 2007905079

ISBN 1-891046-18-7

Printed in the United States of America
9 8 7 6 5 4 3 2 1

Preface

A moral conveys the ethical significance or practical lesson to be learned from a story. It is the principle taught by a legend or tale that portrays what is right or just. What we learn from stories with a moral is of a general or strategic nature rather than a detailed or tactical one. A moral provides a background against which to measure our attitude and behavior. The moral of a well-told story can inspire us by highlighting a virtue to emulate.

The human qualities illustrated in these legends and tales include compassion, courage, determination, humility, loyalty, perseverance, resourcefulness, and unselfishness. Some of them are familiar, such as those about David and Goliath, Robert Bruce, and Roland; most are not as well known. The less familiar ones also deserve our attention. These stories uplift as well as entertain and show that our potential is greater than we think.

TABLE OF CONTENTS

Introduction

A legend is a story or narrative, with some historical basis, often unverifiable, handed down from generation to generation. Much of its content may be fiction, but it has some basis in fact. A legend is usually about people who actually lived, places that really existed, or events that in fact occurred, all embedded in details added later in subsequent retellings .

Legends are considered authentic in the society in which they originated. Frequently, it is difficult to determine the boundary between fact and fiction. Folktales, initially handed down by word of mouth, are not considered historically factual. However, the theme of a folktale may appear in a legend or in time turn into a legend. The boundary between legends and folktales is not well defined.

The distinction between legends and myths is described by Richard Cavendish in the introduction to *Legends of the World*:

> Legends are on a different plane from myths, which are
> imaginative traditions about the nature and destiny of the
> world, the gods, and the human race. In some cases, as in
> the Bible, a people's account of the past begins with
> myth—the creation of the world—and then shades over
> into legends about the founding figures and leaders of the
> nation in its early history. Legends are set on the human
> rather than the divine level, and the central characters of
> legends are human beings, not gods, although they are
> often larger-than-life human beings with supernatural
> powers.

Legends become part of an inherited body of beliefs and values that identify a society. These stories provide insight into the societies that created them. Often legends are passed on to subsequent generations by storytellers.

Many parallels exist among the legends of the world. For example, similarities exist in many stories of the supernatural birth of heroes, including those in which one or both parents were gods. Other similarities are found in the dangers that confronted many of the heroes of legends as children. In the Greek legend of the

Pleiades, for example, the seven daughters of Atlas were changed into stars. In a parallel Iroquois Indian legend, seven young Indian children became a constellation called Oot-kwa-tah by the Iroquois.

These legends and tales are inspiring. They remind us that our lives do not necessarily have to be small lives, and that if we reach out, we can achieve much more than our perceived limitations allow us. These stories not only teach us about moral values, they provide us with examples of behavior to emulate or in some cases to avoid, and they elevate our attitude towards life.

Chapter 1

IMMORTAL / ENDURING

Immortality is not a gift,
Immortality is an achievement;
And only those who strive mightily
Shall possess it.

Edgar Lee Masters, "The Village Atheist," *Spoon River Anthology*

The Gordian Knot—Alexander the Great

A rich, scenic region in western Asia used to be called Phrygia. The center of Phrygia was a plateau in old Asia Minor, dotted with mountains and intersected by several river systems. Phrygians, who were related to the Greeks and were called "freemen" by them, were happy and economically well off. Residents of the mountains had gold mines and marble quarries; residents of the valleys had bountiful vineyards and olive orchards. Those who lived in the hills maintained large flocks of sheep that provided high-quality wool.

For decades, the uncomplicated people of Phrygia did not have a king. None was needed because everyone unselfishly did what was best for all. Eventually, they became more selfish and began to look out for themselves, rather than the rest of the community. The gold miners began to take grapes and olives from their neighbors in the valleys and those with vineyards and olive orchards took sheep from the shepherds in the hills, who, in turn, seized gold that had been mined in the mountains.

A war began, and a happy land became sad. Phrygia had many wise, law-abiding men who were distressed by these conditions. They decided to have a king like other countries to make laws and to punish evildoers. Many considered themselves best qualified to be king and would not give way to another. Finally, one of the wisest suggested that, since they had not been able to select a king, they should ask the gods for advice.

A messenger was sent to the oracle of Apollo, a god of many talents, including prophecy, to present their problem and to seek a solution. The Temple of Apollo was miles away by sea, so many weeks passed before the messenger returned. The wisest men from the mountains, valleys, and hills met to receive the messenger, who admitted that the oracle did not tell him much. The oracle had merely quoted two lines of poetry:

> In a lowly wagon riding, see the king
> Who'll peace to your unhappy country bring.

The gathered crowd was puzzled by the message from the oracle. They didn't understand it but thought that if it came from the oracle, it must be profound. While standing around discussing their dilemma, they saw an oxcart moving slowly down the nearby road.

The cart was carrying a full load of hay and a humble peasant and his wife and child. Everyone in the village knew the peasant, Gordius, the hardest working man in the country. His meager hut with its vine-covered roof was located at the bottom of the hill.

As the cart with its creaking wheels passed by, one of the men said, "In a lowly wagon riding, see the king." Another man quoted the oracle's second line of poetry: "Who'll peace to your unhappy country bring." Suddenly, the gathered men understood the oracle's message and ran to the cart to greet Gordius, who had stopped the cart to find out what was going on. Some shouted, "Hail to our king!" and bowed before him. Others cried out: "Long live the king of the Phrygians." Gordius asked his friends and neighbors what was happening and begged them not to frighten his oxen.

The spokesman for the crowd told Gordius about the message from the oracle. Gordius replied that if the oracle had chosen him as their king, he would be their king. However, he suggested that they start by doing their duty to those who caused this event to happen. He drove his cart to the Temple of Jupiter, their chief god, which overlooked the village. He unhitched his oxen and led them into the temple. He killed the oxen before the altar and collected their blood in a large wooden bowl. Then he prayed while pouring out the blood as an offering of thanks to Jupiter.

Gordius hauled the wagon into the inner temple and gave it to the higher being who makes and unmakes kings. He placed the ox yoke across the end of the wagon pole and tied it with a rope made of bark. He tied the knot so adroitly that the ends of the rope were not visible; no one knew how to untie the knot. Then he began his duties as king. He admitted that he did not know much about being king; nevertheless, he resolved to do his best.

Gordius ruled so well that the difficulties ceased, and the country, including all mountains, valleys, and hills, was at peace and yielded bountiful crops. He made laws that were so just that no one disobeyed them.

All visitors to the village were shown King Gordius's wagon in the Temple of Jupiter. They complimented him on the knot that he had tied and observed that only a great man could have tied such a knot. The oracle of the temple agreed with them, but added that the man who would eventually untie it would be greater. The visitors asked how that could be. The oracle explained that Gordius was king only of Phrygia, a small country, but the man who would untie the knot would have the world for his kingdom.

Many men, including warriors and princes from many lands, tried to untie the Gordian knot without success. The ends of the rope were still hidden; no one could even begin the task. Centuries passed and the cart remained in its place in the inner temple with the yoke tied to the wagon pole. People remembered King Gordius only as the man who had tied the knot.

Eventually, King Alexander from Macedonia crossed the sea into Asia after conquering all of Greece and defeating the King of Persia in battle. Phrygia did not have the army or the courage to oppose him.

Alexander asked about the Gordian knot. Villagers led him into the Temple of Jupiter and showed him the small wagon with the yoke tied to the wagon pole just as Gordius had left it. Alexander asked what the oracle had said about the knot and was told that the man who untied it would have the world for a kingdom.

Alexander looked around the knot several times and could not see the ends of the rope. He raised his sword and cut through the knot with one stroke, causing the yoke to fall to the ground. The young king said that was the way he cut all Gordian knots, and that the world was his kingdom. He moved on with his army to conquer Persia and Egypt, and he built a new city, Alexandria, at the mouth of the Nile. He overran much of India.

Finally, Alexander was told that beyond the lands he had conquered were nothing but deserts, frozen marshes, fields of snow, seas of ice, and tangled forests. Then he, who had never wept before, sat down and wept because there were no more worlds for him to conquer.

Moral: You don't have to be a wealthy, well-educated person to be a good leader. Gordius showed that a common peasant could rule wisely.

Based on: James Baldwin, "The Gordian Knot" and "Why Alexander Wept," *Thirty More Famous Stories Retold*

King Alfred's Lesson in Humility

Some historians consider King Alfred the greatest English king. Alfred devoted himself to the duties of his office and did everything he could to promote the good of his people. He was a warrior, a lawgiver, and a scholar who wrote and translated many books. He was devoid of pride, cruelty, and injustice toward his subjects and his enemies. Alfred was a religious man, a Christian, who encouraged trade and traveled widely.

In 868, when Alfred was twenty, the Danes invaded northern England and in 871 entered Wessex for the first time. That year his brother, King Ethelred, died, and Alfred became King of the West Saxons and Overlord of All England. Alfred battled the Danes off and on until 897, the beginning of a period of peace. Many of the Danes settled in East Anglia. Alfred's battles included sea battles; his navy won many victories at sea, the first of a long series for the Royal Navy.

Alfred considered himself to be under the protection of St. Cuthbert, who he said taught him to fear God and to be righteous toward all men. Alfred ruled well and wisely until his death in 901. He was buried in Winchester.

A tale is told about a time when the Danes surprised Alfred's army and attacked Chippenham in 878. Alfred and his small band hid in the woods and on the moors. During this time, he stayed at the hut of a swineherd, Denewulf, who knew Alfred was the king but did not tell his wife. One day Denewulf's wife placed some cakes in the oven to bake and asked Alfred, who was sitting by the fire mending his bow and arrows, to tend them while she went out to milk the cow.

Unfortunately, King Alfred paid more attention to his weapons and to thinking about how to defeat the Danes than to tending the cakes, and they were burned. When the swineherd's wife returned, she cried out, "There, don't you see the cakes on fire? Then why didn't you turn them? You are glad enough to eat them when they are hot." Some versions of the tale say that she struck the king with a stick in addition to scolding him. Alfred took the scolding lightly; he realized that he had neglected his duties and deserved to incur the wrath of the swineherd's wife.

Moral: Be responsible. If you agree to accept responsibility,
            meet your commitments. Practice humility no matter how
            exalted a position you occupy.

Based on: Hamilton Wright Mabie, "King Alfred,"
           Heroes Every Child Should Know

Croesus Learns that Money Isn't Everything

King Croesus lived in Asia thousands of years ago. His country,
Lydia, was not large, but it was prosperous. Croesus was thought to
be the richest man in the world. Thus the phrase "as rich as
Croesus" was coined. Croesus dressed well and possessed exten-
sive real estate and many works of art. He lacked nothing and was
happy.

One year, Solon, a wise lawmaker from Athens and author of
poetry and verse who was one of the Seven Sages, was traveling
across Asia and visited Croesus in Lydia. Solon was known for his
wisdom. To be referred to as "wise as Solon" was a high compli-
ment for a learned man. Solon visited Croesus at his palace and was
impressed by its large rooms furnished with expensive carpets,
paintings, sculpture, and books. The visitor was also impressed by
the gardens, orchards, and stables.

At dinner the first evening of Solon's visit, Croesus asked his
guest who he thought was the happiest man in the world, thinking
that Solon would say that his host was. Solon thought about the
question briefly and then answered that he thought a poor man
named Tellus who once lived in Athens was the happiest of all men.
Croesus asked Solon why.

Solon replied that his opinion was based on the fact that Tellus
was an honest, hard-working man who had brought up his children
well and had given them a good education. When his children were
grown, Tellus joined the army of Athens and died bravely defend-
ing his country. Solon asked his host if he could think of anyone
who deserved happiness more. Croesus was disappointed but
agreed that Tellus was deserving.

Croesus then asked Solon who he thought ranked second to
Tellus in happiness. Croesus thought for sure that he would be at
least second. Solon replied that he ranked next two young men

from a very poor family in Greece whose father had died when they were quite young. The young men worked hard to maintain the household and to care for their mother, who was ill. They toiled for many years, thinking only of their mother's well-being until she died. Then they transferred their love to Athens, their home city, and served her well for the remainder of their lives.

Croesus became angry and asked Solon why he had such a low opinion of his host, and why he believed that his wealth and power accounted for nothing. Croesus asked why poor working people would be ranked above the richest king in the world in terms of happiness. Solon replied that no one knows whether he is happy or not until he dies. No man can predict what misfortunes he may encounter or whether suffering and unhappiness will take the place of existing grandeur.

Many years later, Cyrus the Great, founder of the Persian empire, formed a large army, conquered every country in his path, and added them to his empire. Croesus with all of his wealth was unable to raise and fund a sufficient army to defend his kingdom. Croesus's army held out for a long time, killing many of Cyrus's men. Finally, however, Croesus was defeated. His palace was burned, his gardens and orchards were destroyed, and his treasured possessions were carted away. Although Cyrus was considered a great warrior and statesman who treated his vanquished enemies humanely, he ordered Croesus to be imprisoned and to be made an example of for other kings who tried to stand in his way.

Cyrus's soldiers took Croesus into custody, roughly dragging him to the marketplace. They piled up wood from the palace that they had destroyed, tied Croesus to a pole in the middle of the pile, and searched for a torch to set the wood on fire. The soldiers looked forward to watching Croesus die in a blazing fire. They asked Croesus what good all his wealth would do him now.

Croesus, bloody and bruised, stood on his funeral pyre with no one to sympathize with him or to pray for him. He remembered the words of Solon that no man can determine if he is happy until he dies. He cried out: "Solon! Solon! Solon!" Cyrus was riding by at the time and heard Croesus cry out. Cyrus rode over to his captive and asked him why he called out the name of Solon. Croesus told of Solon's visit to his palace and what Solon had said about being happy.

Cyrus was deeply affected by the story of Croesus, particularly the thought that no one knows if they are happy or not until they die, and that no man can predict what misfortunes he may encounter. Cyrus wondered if this could also happen to him—to become weak, lose his power, and be helpless when captured by his enemies.

Cyrus realized that he should be kind and lenient to those who are suffering. He decided to treat Croesus as he would have others treat him if their positions were reversed. He gave Croesus his freedom and from then on considered him an honored friend.

Moral: Material wealth is not always a good way of judging happiness. Croesus learned an important lesson from his experience when the soldiers asked him what good all of his wealth was to a captive about to lose his life.

Based on: James Baldwin, "As Rich as Croesus," *Thirty More Famous Stories Retold*

The Sword Of Damocles

King Dionysius of Syracuse was so cruel and unjust that he was called the tyrant of Sicily. He knew that he was universally hated; he lived in fear of being assassinated. He was very rich, lived in a fine palace, and was waited upon hand and foot by a host of servants. One day his friend, Damocles, observed how happy Dionysius must be; he had everything a man could want.

Dionysius asked Damocles if he would like to trade places with him. Damocles replied, "No, not that, oh king! But I think that if I could only have your riches and your pleasures for one day, I would not want any greater happiness."

Dionysius said, "Very well, you shall have them." The following day, Damocles was shown into the palace, and all the servants were told to treat him as their master. He sat down at the table in the banquet hall, where a variety of rich food was placed before him. Nothing that could give him pleasure was denied him: expensive wine, beautiful flower arrangements, enjoyable music, and pleasant aromas. He sat on comfortable cushions and considered himself the happiest man in the world.

Then Damocles looked up. He wondered what was dangling above him, almost touching its head. It was a sharp sword pointed at him, and it was hanging by a single horsehair. He wondered what would happen if the hair broke. Every moment held the danger that it would do so. The smile faded from Damocles's lips. His face became as pale as ashes. His hands trembled as though he had palsy. He could drink no more of the rare wine; he no longer enjoyed the music. He wanted to leave the palace; it didn't matter where he went.

Dionysius asked his friend what was the matter. Damocles responded, "That sword! That sword!" He was so frightened that he couldn't move. Dionysius replied that he knew there was a sword over his head, and that it might fall at any moment. He asked Damocles why that should trouble him; he had a sword hanging over his head all of the time, and he lived in fear every moment of losing his life.

Damocles asked his friend to let him go. He told Dionysius he could see that he had been mistaken; although the rich and powerful are envied, they are not as happy as they seem. Damocles begged to be allowed to return to his little cottage in the mountains. As long as he lived, Damocles never again wanted to be rich or to change places, even for a moment, with the king.

Moral: Risk accompanies the easy living of the rich and powerful.
   Be careful what you wish for; you might get it.

Based on: James Baldwin, "The Sword of Damocles,"
   Fifty Famous Stories Retold

The King and His Hawk—Genghis Khan

Some Mongolian legends relate that young Genghis Khan was a prince (khan) and others that he was a god (burkhan), a son of the sky god Khormusta-tengri who came down to earth. He became a great military leader who led his army into China and Persia, conquered many countries, and became king during the late 1100s and early 1200s.

One tale of King Genghis Khan takes place in Mongolia when he was home from the wars and hunting in the woods with friends.

The hunting party, accompanied by hounds and servants, was relaxing and having a good time. The king's favorite hawk perched on his right wrist. His hawk was a well-trained hunter that climbed high in the sky to bring down game birds or swooped down to the ground to attack rabbits.

The king and his party had hunted all day without success. Disappointed, they headed toward home early in the evening. The main body of the party took the shortest way home; the king went home by a longer route through a valley between two majestic mountains. His hawk had left his wrist and had flown away. The king knew that his pet hunter could find its way home. The day had been very warm, and the king was thirsty.

The last time that Genghis Khan had taken this route home, he had seen a spring next to the path. Unfortunately, the long, hot summer had dried up many of the mountain brooks. Eventually, he saw some water trickling over the edge of a rock. He knew that a spring was located farther up the mountain. During the rainy season, a swiftly flowing stream poured down the hillside. Now it was reduced to one drop at a time.

The king climbed down from his horse, took a small silver cup from his saddlebag, and held it to catch the falling drops. It took a long time to fill the cup, but at last it was almost full; he put the cup to his lips to drink. He heard the flapping of wings and the cup was knocked from his hands. The water spilled on the ground. The king looked up and saw his pet hawk, which flew around him a few times and then perched on a rock by the spring.

The king picked up the cup and held it under the drops coming off of the rock. When the cup was half full, he lifted it toward his mouth to drink. Again, the hawk swooped down and knocked the cup from his grasp. The king began to get angry. He tried a third time, and again the hawk prevented him from drinking the water. He became very angry and yelled at the bird and threatened to wring its neck.

Genghis Khan filled the cup one more time but before lifting it to his lips, he drew his sword. He told the hawk that this was the last time, but his pet again knocked the cup out of his hand. This time, the king was ready and struck the hawk with his sword as he passed. The bird lay bleeding and dying at the feet of his master.

When the king looked for his cup, he found that it had fallen in the rocks beyond his reach. He decided to climb up the hillside and drink from the spring. He became thirstier as he struggled up the hill. When he reached the spring, he saw that a dead poisonous snake almost filled the pool. The king stopped, forgot his thirst, and could only think of the dead hawk lying on the ground below him.

The King realized that his pet hunter had saved his life, and he asked himself how he had repaid him. He had killed a good friend that was only trying to help him. He climbed down the side of the hill, picked up the bird, gently placed it in his saddlebag, and rode home. On the way home, he realized that he had learned an important lesson that day: action taken in anger may be regretted later when times are calmer.

Moral: Never act in anger. Counting to ten before acting is
      good advice.

Based on: James Baldwin, "The King and His Hawk,"
      Fifty Famous Stories Retold

Chapter 2

NOTABLE / LOYAL

There are loyal hearts, there are spirits brave,
There are souls that are pure and true;
Then give to the world the best you have,
And the best will come back to you.

Mary Ainge De Vere, "Madeline Bridges," *Life's Mirror,* Stanza I

The Paynim's Promise

Centuries ago, the Moors crossed the Mediterranean Sea, invaded Spain, and took control of most of southern Spain. During the ensuing warfare, the Spanish General Narvaez captured the Moorish town of Medina Antequara. He maintained a garrison there and used the city as a base of operations for plundering neighboring districts of Grenada to provision his army.

One morning, Narvaez dispatched a large body of cavalry to pillage the surrounding area. The raid began early and by sunrise had penetrated far into enemy countryside. The officer commanding the detachment, who rode well in front of his men, encountered a young Moor who had lost his way in the darkness and appeared to be returning home. The young man fought the Spanish horsemen boldly but was soon overcome.

The cavalrymen returned to Antequara, bringing with them their captive, a handsome young man in his mid-twenties with a dignified appearance. He was dressed in a flowing mulberry-colored silk robe, richly decorated in the Moorish style, and was mounted on a fine Arabian horse.

Narvaez judged him to be an important cavalier. He asked his name and was told that his prisoner was the son of the Alcayde of Ronda, a Moor of high distinction and a relentless enemy of the Spaniards. When Narvaez questioned the prisoner, the young man was unable to reply. He began to cry and was choked by sobs that appeared to come from a heart deeply overcome with grief.

Narvaez told the young man he was surprised that a cavalier of good race with a noble father should be so downcast and weeping like a woman. He reminded him that one with the appearance of a good knight and a brave soldier should not be so saddened by the chances of war. The youth told the general he was not weeping because he had been taken prisoner but was suffering from a much deeper sorrow, compared with which his being a prisoner was of no consequence.

Narvaez, moved by the young man's seriousness and pitying his situation, asked him to confide in him the cause of his sorrow. The prisoner, struck by the general's sympathy, sighed and replied: "Lord Governor, I have long loved a lady, daughter of the alcayde of a nearby fortress. Many times I have fought in her honor against the men of your race. In time, the lady returned my affection, and declared herself willing to be my wife; I was on my way to her when, by chance, I encountered your horsemen and fell into their hands. Thus I have lost not only my liberty, but all the happiness of my life, which I believed I held in my hands. If this does not seem to you worthy of tears, I know not for what purpose they are given to the eyes of man, or how to make you understand my misery."

Narvaez was deeply affected by his prisoner's story and decided to do what he could to ease his predicament. The general told the young man that since he was a cavalier of good family, if he would pledge his word to return to Antequara, he would be given permission to visit his beloved to acquaint her with the reason for his absence that day.

The Moor accepted his captor's offer, assuring Narvaez he would return. He arrived that evening at the fortress where his lady lived. He entered the garden and gave the agreed-upon signal to meet her at their trysting place. She arrived immediately, expressing her surprise that he had not come earlier. When he told her what had happened, his beloved was cast down into the deepest grief. He tried every means of consoling her, without success. Finally, with the arrival of midnight, he reminded her of his promise to return to captivity.

The young Moor told his loved one that although he had lost his own liberty, he did not want to place her in a position of danger. He told her they must wait patiently until a ransom could be paid to free him, and then he would return to her.

The young woman said he had given many indications of his love for her, enforced now by his concern for her safety. She told him that she would be most ungrateful if she did not share his captivity, and that she would accompany him to the Spanish prison. She added that if he must be a slave, she would be also.

The young lady asked her maid to fetch her jewel case. When she received it, she mounted the horse behind her lover. They rode all night and arrived at Antequara in the morning, where they presented themselves to Narvaez, who was as moved by the loyalty of the young woman as he was by the honor and fidelity of the Moor. He immediately gave both their liberty and loaded them with many gifts. He gave them permission to return to their homes and provided an escort to accompany them.

The adventure, the love of the lady, the loyalty of the Moor, and the generosity of the Spanish commander were celebrated by the noble Saracens of Granada. These events were chronicled by their annalists and poets. Although this tale is by nature a romance, it has the additional merit of being true.

Moral: Loyalty is an extremely important quality.
　　　　Putting your safety at risk for another is heroic.

Based on: Lewis Spence, "The Paynim's Promise,"
　　　　Legends and Romances of Spain

Regulus Keeps His Word

Three Punic Wars were fought between Rome and Carthage. Rome considered itself the protector of Italy and neighboring Sicily. Carthage invaded Sicily to increase its control in the western Mediterranean. In 256 BC, the ninth year of the First Punic War, Roman general and consul Marcus Atilius Regulus landed an army on Carthaginian territory after shattering the Carthaginian fleet. Eventually, the other Roman consul was recalled, leaving Regulus to finish the war.

After Regulus defeated them decisively near Carthage, the Carthaginians were inclined to sue for peace. Unfortunately, the victor's terms were so harsh the Carthaginians decided to continue the war. In 255 BC, Regulus was soundly defeated and taken prisoner by General Xanthippus of Sparta, an ally of Carthage.

Regulus was imprisoned in Carthage for five years. He was lonely in prison and dreamed frequently about his wife and children, whom he had little hope of ever seeing again. He regretted being in prison, but he felt that he had served his country to the best of his ability. He knew that the Romans were gaining ground, and that the Carthaginians were apprehensive about being defeated. Carthage was running out of mercenaries and probably could not hold out much longer against Rome.

One day, the rulers of Carthage visited Regulus in prison and told him they would like to make peace with the Romans. They said if the Roman consuls knew how the war was going, they would be inclined to make peace. They offered to free Regulus so that he could return to Rome, with two conditions. First, they instructed

Regulus to tell his countrymen about the battles he had lost and to make it clear that Rome had not gained anything by the war. They asked him to seek peace and an exchange of prisoners. Second, they made Regulus promise that if the Romans would not agree to peace, he would return to Carthage.

Regulus agreed with their conditions and promised to return to prison in Carthage if his countrymen could not be persuaded to make peace. They let him go, trusting that he would keep his word. When he returned to Rome, he was greeted warmly by the people; his family was overjoyed to see him. The city fathers asked him about the progress of the war.

Regulus told the Roman consuls he had been sent from Carthage to make peace and to ask for an exchange of prisoners. However, he counseled that it would not be wise to make peace. Certainly, he admitted, the Romans had been beaten in a few battles, but they were gaining ground every day. The people of Carthage were afraid of losing the war. Regulus suggested that if they fought the war a little longer, Carthage would be defeated.

To the consternation of his family, Regulus told the consuls he would leave Rome for Carthage the following day. He told the consuls he had promised to return to prison in Carthage if peace were not declared. They begged him to stay and offered to send someone else in his place. He asked them if a Roman was not expected to keep his word. Regulus said tearful goodbyes to his family and traveled to Carthage, where he was imprisoned and tortured to death. Regulus was a man whose courage was much revered by his countrymen.

Moral: Be a man or woman of your word. Regulus kept his word even though it meant forfeiting his life in the service of his country.

Based on: James Baldwin, "The Story of Regulus,"
Favorite Tales of Long Ago

Dick Whittington's Tale

Dick Whittington did not know his parents. They either died or abandoned him with the parish of Taunton Dean in Somersetshire, England. He ran away at the age of seven because of the cruel treatment of the orphanage nurse. He walked around the country, living on charity. Whittington grew into a sturdy youth. Eventually he was threatened with whippings if he continued his idle life. He decided to go to London, where he heard there was opportunity.

Whittington did not know the way, so he followed the transport wagons. At night, he rubbed down the horses, and the drivers gave him supper. When they arrived in London, the drivers, considering him a potentially troublesome hanger-on, told him to leave the inn and to look for a job. They gave him a silver fourpence piece for his troubles. He wandered about London in tattered clothes. He knew no one, and few gave him anything.

Whittington soon had spent the fourpence, and his stomach craved food. He resolved to starve rather than steal, however. After two days without food, he was weary and faint but made his way to the home of a merchant in Leadenhall Street. He asked for food but was denied by the ill-natured cook, who threatened to throw him into the kennel. He lay on the ground, able to go no farther. Whittington was found that way by Mr. Fitz-Warren, the owner of the house, when he came home from the Royal Exchange.

Mr. Fitz-Warren called Whittington a lazy, idle fellow and asked him what he wanted; he told Whittington if he did not leave immediately, he would have him sent to the House of Correction. Whittington got up, falling several times due to faintness for lack of food. He made a bow, and told Mr. Fitz-Warren he was a poor country fellow in a starving condition who would refuse no labor, even if it were only for food.

This raised a Christian compassion in the merchant, who then, needing a kitchen servant, told one of the servants to take the young man in. He gave orders to feed Whittington and give him directions about his employment. This was the first step of Providence to raise him up to a greater position than he could have dreamed of.

Early on, Whittington met with many difficulties. The servants made fun of him, and the ill-natured cook told him: "You are to come under me, so look sharp; clean the spit and dripping pan, make the fires, and nimbly do all other scullery work that I may set you about, or else I will break your head with my ladle, and kick you about like a football."

Whittington suffered under this treatment, but it was better that starving. His ray of hope was Miss Alice, his master's daughter, who, hearing that her father had hired a new servant, came to see him; she ordered that he be kindly treated. She talked with Whittington about his life and found him honest and sincere. She obtained some cast-off clothing for him and gave her parents a favorable opinion of him. They observed, "He looks like a service-able fellow to do kitchen drudgery, run errands, clean the shoes, and do chores that the other servants consider beneath them." A bed was prepared for him in the garret.

Whittington was pleased with his opportunities, and he showed great diligence in his work. He got up early and stayed up late; he left nothing undone that he could do. Unfortunately, being under the control of the cook, his working conditions were not always favorable. She used her authority beyond reason; he had to bear patiently many a rap on the head. The more he tried to dissuade her from being cruel, the more she insulted and abused him. Also, she frequently complained about him and tried to get him turned out of the house. He was saved by Miss Alice who knew of the cook's ill-will and spoke up in his favor.

Whittington's other problem was the large number of rats and mice in the garret where he slept. They ran over his face and kept him awake with their squeaking. Concerning his first problem, he lived in hope that the cook would soon leave, marry, or die. He decided a cat would help solve his problem with the rats and mice.

A merchant who stayed overnight had given Whittington a penny for cleaning and polishing his shoes. On the next errand Whittington was asked to run, he saw a woman along the road with a cat under her arm. He asked the price of it; she told him sixpence for a good mouser. He told her he had only a penny, and she let him have it. He kept the cat in a box in the attic; she was very effective in eliminating his rodent problem. Unfortunately his problem in the kitchen remained for many years.

Mr. Fitz-Warren had a custom of calling his servants together when he sent out a merchant ship and asking them all to venture something, to try their fortune. He hoped this might cause God to give a greater blessing to his endeavors. The servants did not have to pay either freight or customs charges. All the servants except Whittington came with something to sell, according to their abilities. Miss Alice noticed Whittington's absence and supposed that his poverty prevented him from coming.

Whittington made several excuses but was finally prevailed upon to join the gathering. He fell upon his knees, asking them not to jeer at a poor, simple fellow. He told them the only possession he had was an effective mouser cat for which he had paid a penny.

Miss Alice offered to put something down for him; her father reminded her that he must venture something of his own. He was ordered to fetch his cat, which he did with great reluctance, thinking that nothing could come of it. Tearfully, he delivered his cat to the master of the ship *Unicorn*, which was to sail down to Blackwall before proceeding on her voyage.

The cook, when she was not scolding Whittington, jeered at his grand adventure with the cat, and generally made his life so uncomfortable that he grew weary of enduring it. Expecting little relief from his living conditions, he resolved to leave rather than live in misery. He packed up his bundle overnight and left early on All Hallow's Day, intending to roam about the country. As he passed through Moorfields, he had second thoughts, and his resolution began to fail. He continued on to Holloway and Bun Hill, where he sat down to consider the matter. All of a sudden the bells of Bow Church began to ring.

Listening to the peal of the bells, Whittington fancied they called him back from his intended roamings and promised him good fortune. He imagined they were telling him:

> Turn again, Whittington
> Lord Mayor of London.

This happy thought helped change his mind. It was still early; he realized that he could get back to London before the family stirred. He walked swiftly and, having left the door ajar, crept quietly into the house and returned to his drudgery.

The good ship *Unicorn* was driven onto the Barbary Coast by contrary winds. The Moors were unknown to the English but treated them courteously. The Master traded with them. The Moors looked at samples of the wares on the deck of the *Unicorn* and were so pleased that the king asked the Master to come to his palace.

The Moors' entertainment, according to custom, was held on the floor, which was covered with carpets interwoven with gold and silver, upon which they sat cross-legged. Low tables were laden with various dishes. As the scent of rich food spread through the room, a swarm of mice and rats began to devour the food that had been served. The Master was surprised; he asked the noblemen if they were not offended by these vermin.

The noblemen replied, "His Majesty would give half his revenue to be rid of them; they are offensive, not only at the table but also in his living and sleeping chambers. The Master, remembering Whittington's cat, told the Moors that he had an English beast on board the ship that would rid the palace of them quickly.

The king, anxious to be rid of the rats and mice that spoiled his pleasure, wanted to see this creature. The king said, "For such a service, I will load your ship with gold, diamonds, and pearls." This generous offer motivated the Master to see if he could obtain even more by enhancing the cat's merits. He told the king: "She is the most admirable creature in the world, and I cannot spare her, for she keeps my ships free of vermin. Otherwise, they would destroy all of my goods."

His Majesty would not be denied, saying, "No price shall keep us apart." Whittington's cat was sent for. The tables were spread, and the rats and mice came as before. When the cat was placed on the table, she fell to her task and killed all the rats and mice in short order. Then she came purring and curling her tail to the king and queen as if she were asking for a reward for her services. They admired her and were thankful for the service that she provided.

The Moorish king was so pleased with the cat, especially when the Master told him that she was with young and would stock the whole country, that he paid ten times more for the cat than for all of the freight he purchased. The *Unicorn* sailed with a fair wind and arrived safely at Blackwall, as one of the richest ships ever to enter an English port.

The Master took the case of jewels with him, not trusting for them to be left on board. He presented his bill of lading to Mr. Fitz-Warren, who praised God for such a successful voyage. When he called all the servants to give them their due, the Master revealed the case of jewels, the sight of which surprised them. On being told it was all for Whittington's cat, Fitz-Warren said, "God forbid that I should deprive him of a farthing of it." He sent for him by the title of Mr. Whittington, who was in the kitchen cleaning pots and pans.

When told that the master had asked to see him, Whittington made several excuses not to go. Finally, he came to the doorway and hesitated, until the master told him to come in and sit down in front of all the servants. He did not know what they wanted with him; he hoped they were not going to taunt him. Mr. Fitz-Warren said, "Indeed, Mr. Whittington, we are serious with you, for, in estate at this moment, you are a wealthier man than I." He then gave Whittington the vast riches, amounting to three hundred thousand pounds.

When they were able to persuade Whittington of his good fortune, he fell on his knees and praised Almighty God. Then turning to his master, he laid the case of jewels at his feet. Mr. Fitz-Warren said, "No, Mr. Whittington, God forbid that I should take as much as a ducat from you." Then Whittington turned to Miss Alice, but she also refused it. Bowing low, he said to her, "Miss Alice, whenever you make a choice of a husband, I will give you a fortune."

Mr. Whittington shared some of his bounty with his fellow servants, even giving the cook one hundred pounds for her portion. When she apologized that she had acted in passion, he forgave her. He also distributed his windfall liberally to the ship's crew.

Haberdashers, tailors, and seamstresses were set to work to make clothes suitable for Mr. Whittington's new status in life. In his new clothes, he was a comely person; Miss Alice began to look in his direction. When her father observed this, he encouraged it.

Mr. Fitz-Warren took Mr. Whittington to the Royal Exchange to observe the customs of the merchants, who welcomed him into their society. Soon a match was proposed between him and Miss Alice. He excused himself on account of the meanness of his birth. That objection was removed by his present worth.

The marriage was agreed upon, and the Lord Mayor, the Aldermen, and the principal merchants of the City of London were invited to the wedding. After the honeymoon, Whittington's father-in-law asked him what employment he would undertake. He replied that he intended to be a merchant. They joined together in a partnership and grew immensely rich.

Soon, Whittington was chosen to be sheriff and acquitted himself well in that office. Eventually, the words that the bells of Bow Church had rung out were fulfilled. In the twenty-first year of the reign of King Richard II, Whittington was chosen mayor and was knighted by the King. He served three times as Mayor of London. In his name and in the name of Dame Alice, his wife, he founded diverse charities in remembrance of the gratitude he owed Almighty God for having raised him up from so mean a creature to so great a fortune and dignity. After his death, his executors continued his good work.

Moral: Be humble, forgiving, and charitable when the opportunity presents itself. Be patient in adversity and thankful for good fortune.

Based on: Milton Rugoff, "Dick Whittington,"
    A Harvest of World Folk Tales

Damon and Pythias

As a young man, Pythias did something to offend Dionysius, tyrant of the city-state of Syracuse in the fourth century BC. For his offense, he was dragged away to prison and sentenced to death. He wanted to see his mother and father before he died, but he was a long way from home. He begged Dionysius to be allowed to go home and visit his loved ones; he promised to return to give up his life. The tyrant laughed at Pythias and asked how he would know that he would keep his promise. Dionysius thought Pythias only wanted to cheat him and save his life.

Pythias's friend Damon spoke up and offered to be put in prison in his friend's place. Damon begged that Pythias be allowed to travel to his home country to put his affairs in order and to say farewell to his family and friends. Damon knew Pythias as a man of his word who would return as he had promised. He offered to die in his friend's place if Pythias had not returned by an appointed date. Dionysius was surprised that anyone would make such an offer. He agreed to let Pythias return home, and he ordered Damon to be imprisoned.

Weeks passed, and Pythias did not return to Syracuse. The day set for Damon to die drew near. Dionysius told the prison guards to watch Damon closely in case he attempted to escape, but he did not try. Damon had the utmost faith in his friend. He knew that if Damon did not return, it would be due to circumstances beyond his control.

At last, the appointed day came and then the hour of execution. Damon was prepared to die. His belief in the honor of his friend never wavered. Because of his love for his friend, he did not grieve. As the jailer came to lead him to his death, Damon saw Pythias standing in the doorway. He had been delayed by storms and a ship-wreck. He feared that he was too late. Pythias placed himself in the hands of the jailer. He was relieved that he had made it in time to save Damon.

Dionysius was not so much of a tyrant that he could not see good in others. He felt that men who loved and trusted each other, such as Damon and Pythias, should not suffer unjustly. He set them both free and said that he would give his entire wealth to have one such friend.

Moral: Loyalty to a friend is admirable. Having the honor to keep one's word even though the consequences are dire is even more admirable.

Based on: James Baldwin, "Damon and Pythias," *Favorite Tales of Long Ago*

The Loyalty of Penelope

One of the bravest and most daring of the young Greek chieftains who fought against Troy was Ulysses, the son of King Laertes of the Ionian island of Ithaca. Although he was esteemed as a skillful fighter, he was admired even more for his shrewd counsel.

Ulysses had not gone willingly to war with Troy. He would have preferred to stay home with his beautiful wife, Penelope, and his young son, Telemachus. He would rather have wielded the plow in his vineyards and orchards than the sword and spear in the tur-moil of battle. However, the princes of Greece had requested his services, and he did not want to appear cowardly.

Laertes encouraged his son to do his duty and prayed that Athena, the goddess of wisdom, would look out for him and bring him home safely. Penelope promised to keep his palace safe and fulfill his responsibilities until he returned. Ulysses sailed away to war. The war with Troy, ending in a lengthy siege, lasted for ten years, although Ulysses only participated toward the end of that span. After the defeat of Troy, each Greek chieftain embarked in his own ships to return to his native land.

Ulysses had fond memories of Penelope and Telemachus and yearned to see them again. He longed for the rugged mountains and scenic shores of Ithaca. He knew that Penelope would have taken care of his responsibilities, and that his young son would be sturdy and accomplished. He encouraged his men to spread all of the sails and to row hard.

Ulysses's ships were barely at sea when they encountered violent storms. They were blown far off course at the mercy of the winds. His captains lost their bearings and were no longer sure of the direction to Ithaca. After visiting numerous little-known regions, he lost all of his ships and men and was washed up on the shores of the island of Calypso. After eight years, he was released but wrecked his ship on the shores of Phaeacia. The Phaeacians treated him kindly and sent him home in one of their ships.

After the defeat of Troy, the other Greek chieftains arrived home one by one over several years. Word of their return circulated around Greece, but no one knew whether Ulysses and his men were living or dead. Old Laertes, loyal Penelope, and young Telemachus gazed out to sea looking for Ulysses's ships. In time, however, Laertes feared that his son was at bottom of the sea and no longer stood on the shore looking seaward.

The men and women of Ithaca had the same fear as Laertes — that too much time had passed to hope for the return of Ulysses. Penelope did not give up hope; every day she set his place at the table, hung his jacket by his chair, and polished his great bow that hung in the dining hall to keep it supple.

Ten years passed with no word of Ulysses. Telemachus had become a young man, tall and well-mannered. Penelope's queenly beauty had not faded with time; grace and dignity had been added to her youthful loveliness. Her qualities were known throughout Greece. Men talked about the charms of her face and figure, her sweetness, and her noble mind. They counseled her to remarry, convinced that her husband wasn't going to return. They advised her to marry one of the young chieftains of Greece and share with him the kingdom of Ithaca and its wealth.

Aggressive suitors began to arrive in Ithaca. The first to arrive was Antinous, a young insolent, overbearing chieftain. Next came Agelaus, a vain prince, preoccupied with his clothes and his manners. The third was Leocritus, a fat, pompous merchant who talked only about his wealth. Other suitors followed.

All of these suitors along with their belongings and servants moved into the palace without invitation. They expected treatment as honored guests. The suitors reminded Penelope that it was not the custom of the country for a widow to wait a long time to wed again. Each suitor told her of his good qualities, noble family, powerful friends, and wealth. They assured her if she chose among them, the rest of them would leave.

Penelope told them she was certain that Ulysses was still alive, and that she must hold his kingdom for him until he returned—as she had promised. They insisted that she make her choice among them. She asked for another month to wait for Ulysses. She told them that in her loom she had a partially finished web of soft linen she was weaving to make a shroud for Laertes, who was very old and would not live much longer. She promised to choose between them if her husband did not return before the web was finished.

They asked Penelope if she intended to work on the shroud every day. She agreed to sit at her loom and weave the shroud daily. She told them that it would be unfortunate if Laertes died before he could be wrapped in his shroud.

Meanwhile, the suitors made themselves at home in the palace, feasted in the great hall, and consumed provisions that had been stored away for the return of Ulysses. They helped themselves to vegetables and flowers from the garden and fruit from the orchards. They drank freely from the wine cellar and were insolent to Penelope's servants and friends. The people of Ithaca were terrified by their lawlessness.

Every day, Penelope would sit at her loom and weave. In the evening, she would call attention to how much she had added to the length of the web. Every night, while her suitors slept, she unraveled all of the threads that she had woven that day. Thus, although she kept busy at her loom, the shroud remained unfinished.

As long as the wine and the food held out, the suitors did not seem to mind that the web had not gotten longer. When the suitors asked Penelope when the web would be finished, she pointed out how fine and soft it was. She reminded them that work with such delicate meshes could not be hurried.

Agelaus, however, was not satisfied with her explanations. In the middle of night, he crept down the hallway to the weaving room. He observed Penelope busily unraveling the work she had done that day, while whispering the name of Ulysses over and over. The spy returned quietly to his sleeping quarters, determined to confront the mistress of the palace the next day.

Agelaus told the other suitors at breakfast about his discovery. When Penelope entered the dining hall, she was greeted with laughter. They told her that now that she had been found out, she must finish the web that day and choose between them that evening. They would wait no longer. She asked for one additional day, then the shroud would be finished. If they would wait until tomorrow evening when the moon was full, she would give them her answer. They agreed, but said they would not wait a moment longer.

The next afternoon, the suitors were assembled in the great hall as usual, but they ate, drank, sang, and were rowdy as never before. They were so boisterous that the shields and swords hung on the walls rattled. At the peak of their revelry, Telemachus and Eumaeus, his father's most trusted servant, entered the great hall and began to take down the shields and swords from the walls.

Telemachus carried away the swords, and Eumaeus took down the shields. Telemachus told his trusted servant to leave the great bow of Ulysses on the wall because his mother polished and suppled it every day. As they were going out with the last load, Antinous asked what they were doing. Telemachus told him they were putting the weapons in the great chest in the treasure room because they were becoming tarnished by smoke and dust. One of the younger suitors commented that Telemachus seemed uncommonly cheerful. Leocritus sneered that maybe he was expecting his father.

At that moment, a strange beggar entered the courtyard. He was dressed in rags, his feet were bare, and his hands trembled as he walked slowly towards the doorway of the great hall. Some of the servants laughed at his poverty and asked him to leave. Others pitied him and suggested that they treat him kindly.

An old greyhound, Argos, was lying by the kitchen door. Twenty years earlier, he had been a swift hunting dog, Ulysses's loyal companion. Now, he was old, helpless, and ignored. When Argos saw the beggar walking slowly through the yard, he raised his head to look at him with his failing eyes. A light came into his eyes, and he wagged his tail and tried to get up. He looked lovingly into the beggar's face and let out a low growl. The beggar patted the dog's head and said, "Argos, my old friend." Having heard the growl, Antinous asked what was ailing the dog. Agelaus said that maybe he was mourning the loss of his mistress. All of the suitors laughed.

The beggar stood in the doorway. Leocritus asked who the stranger was, pushing himself among his betters. Another suitor called the beggar old rags, threw a crust at his head, and asked him if he knew that this was the king's palace. He told him to leave. Eumaeus, trying to appear harsh, also asked him to leave. The beggar asked to speak with the son of Ulysses. Telemachus, frowning and appearing to be angry, told the beggar that he was the son of Ulysses and to make his story short.

The beggar observed to Telemachus that he was strong and fair and had his entire life ahead of him, whereas he was old and had fallen on hard times. The distressed beggar asked for pity. In a low voice, he asked Telemachus if he had removed all of the weapons as he had requested and if they were safe in the great chest. Telemachus said that, except for the great bow, they were. Telemachus and Eumaeus asked if this was the time to strike.

Antinous saw the beggar say something to Telemachus and asked what he had said. Leocritus suggested that they let the beggar stay and have some fun with him. He asked the beggar if he had come to claim the hand of Penelope also. The beggar did not answer.

The stately Penelope came down the stairs surrounded by her maids and servants. The suitors called out that she had come to fulfill her promise. Penelope asked her son why the beggar was being treated so poorly. Telemachus told his mother that he was merely a wandering beggar who might have news of his father. She wanted to hear his news but she insisted that the beggar must rest and be fed and received politely, like all guests to the palace. She asked a servant to seat the poor man on the far side of the room and asked her son to serve him food and drink personally.

Penelope asked one of her young maids to bring a bowl of water to wash the beggar's feet. The young maid refused because she was too proud. The old nurse who had cared for Ulysses in his youth offered to do what the queen had asked. The nurse brought towels and warm water in a bowl and kneeled on the stone floor in front of the stranger. Suddenly, observing a scar on his knee that she knew to be her master's, she cried out and overturned the bowl. Only the stranger heard her cry out. To avoid suspicion, she observed loudly how awkward she had become in her old age. She went to refill the bowl.

When she returned, the beggar whispered how discreet and wise she had been. He told her that he knew that she had recognized his boyhood scar, but to keep it a secret because the time of vengeance was near. She told Ulysses she knew that he would return. When the shrewd old nurse left the great hall, she muttered complaints about the troublesome beggar.

The man in rags was indeed Ulysses who had come ashore that morning in a small boat. He had first made himself known to Eumaeus and then to his son, but to no one else. He had ordered them to remove the weapons from the great hall.

The suitors gathered around the feast table and were more raucous than before. They shouted for Penelope to join them and told her that she could wait until tomorrow to hear the beggar's story. They reminded her that the moon was full, and that she must fulfill her promise and choose among them. They added that even if Ulysses lived, he would never enter this palace again.

Vain Agelaus asked Penelope to choose him because not even Apollo could match him for grace of form and figure. Rich Leocritus suggested that she choose him so that the treasures of the land and sea would be hers. Insolent Antinous insisted that she select him because she dare not cause his displeasure, and that she would be his whether she chose him or not.

Penelope suggested that she was not fit to decide a question of this magnitude. She suggested leaving it to the gods. She pointed to the great war bow of Ulysses hanging on the wall and said that she would choose the one among them who could attach the bowstring and shoot an arrow the farthest. The suitors all agreed and asked Telemachus to hand them the bow.

Antinous tried first and struggled to bend it. He threw it on the ground and said that only a giant could bend it. One by one, all of the suitors attempted to bend the bow and attach the bowstring. They all failed. Agelaus sneered that now that the beggar has had his feet washed, maybe he might like to try to string the bow.

Ulysses, in his beggar's clothes, rose from his chair, walked haltingly to the head of the hall, and lifted the great bow. He looked with fond memories at the polished and supple bow and commented that he had had a bow like it in his younger days. He took the bow and pretended to struggle with it. Antinous cried out that he had seen enough. He struck Ulysses in the face and told him to leave the company of his betters.

Suddenly, a great change came over Ulysses. Without effort, he strung the great bow, rose to his full height, and shook off his beggar's rags. He appeared in his own likeness, clad in armor from head to foot, every inch a king. Penelope cried out, "Oh Ulysses, Ulysses," and fainted into the arms of the old nurse.

The suitors were speechless in their amazement and tried to escape from the hall. The arrows of Ulysses were swift and sure; not one missed its mark. He cried out that he had now avenged himself on those who had eaten up his substance and attempted to destroy his home.

The next day, Ulysses sat in the great hall with his wife and son and the people of his household, and related the story of his long wanderings on the sea. Penelope told how she had faithfully kept the kingdom for him as she had promised, despite much hardship. She went into the weaving room and returned with a roll of fine white cloth and told Ulysses that this was the web that she had been weaving as a shroud for his father. She told him she had promised that on its completion, she would choose a husband. She told Ulysses that she chose him.

Moral: Everything comes to him or her who is loyal and waits.
       Even when things appear to be hopeless, hope still exists.

Based on: James Baldwin, "Penelope's Web,"
Thirty More Famous Stories Retold

Chapter 3

SELF-DETERMINED / RESPONSIBLE

Some minds seem almost to create themselves,
Springing up under every disadvantage
And working their solitary but irresistible way
Through a thousand obstacles.

Washington Irving, "Roscoe," *The Sketchbook of Geoffrey Crayon, Gent.*

The Sacrifice of Aliquipiso

An Oneida Indian village was raided by a band of Mingoes from the north. Mingoes listened to bad spirits and killed everyone and destroyed everything in their path. Oneida women and children abandoned their lodges and fled to the large rocks in the hills where their braves protected them. The savage marauders searched for days without success for the people of the village.

The Oneidas ran out of food; they feared that if they foraged and hunted, they would be killed. Meeting in council, the warriors and chiefs could think of no solution to their problem. If they remained behind the rocks on the cliff, they would starve; if they ventured out, they would be enslaved or brutally murdered.

A young maiden, Aliquipiso, visited the council of braves and sachems and told them about an idea the Good Spirits had given to her. They told her that if the rocks high on the cliff were rolled into the valley below, everything there would be destroyed. The Good Spirits also told Aliquipiso that if she would lure the plundering Mingoes to the valley below the rocks, they would be killed also. The braves and chiefs were relieved to hear of a solution to their plight. They gave her a necklace of white wampum, made her a princess of the Oneida Nation, and reminded her that she was loved by the Great Spirit.

Aliquipiso left her people in the middle of the night and climbed down from the cliff. The next morning, Mingo scouts found a young maiden wandering lost in the forest. They led Aliquipiso back to the abandoned Oneida village, where they attempted to get her to reveal the hiding place of the Oneidas. They tortured her, but she held out for a long time and won the respect of her captors. Finally, she told the Mingoes that she would lead them to her people. When darkness came, Aliquipiso led her captors to the base of the cliff. Two strong Mingo braves held her in their grasp and were prepared to kill her at the first hint of deception.

The Mingo warriors gathered around Aliquipiso, thinking that she was going to show them an opening into a large cave in the cliff. Suddenly, she lifted her head and let out a piercing cry. Above them, the starving Oneida braves pushed the large boulders over the cliff, at her signal. The Mingoes did not have time to get out the way and were crushed under the rocks, along with the Oneida heroine.

Aliquipiso, who was buried near the scene of her courageous sacrifice, was mourned by the Oneidas for many moons. The Great Spirit used her hair to create woodbine, called "running hairs" by the Iroquois, the climbing vine that protects old trees. The Great Spirit changed her body into honeysuckle, which was called "the blood of brave women" by the Oneidas.

Moral: Sacrificing time and effort for others is admirable;
      sacrificing your life is heroic.

Emerson Klees, "The Sacrifice of Aliquipiso,"
More Legends and Stories

Catherine, Sly Country Lass

One day a farmer was cultivating his vineyard with a hoe and struck something hard. It appeared to be a mortar used for crushing and grinding with a pestle. He bent over, picked it up, and brushed off the dirt. It was solid gold; he could see no impurities in it. He thought to himself that only a king could own something as fine as this. He decided to present it to his king, who, in all likelihood, would reward him handsomely.

The farmer returned home and showed the gold mortar to his daughter, Catherine, and told her of his intention to present it to the king. She agreed that it was impressive but told her father that the king would find something wrong with it, since something was missing. Her father asked what was wrong with it; what was missing? Catherine told her father that the king would like the large, beautiful mortar but would ask, "Where is the pestle?" The farmer disagreed, saying that the king did not think like she did.

The farmer carried the mortar to the king's palace. The guards weren't going to let him in until he explained that he had a wonderful gift for the king. "Your majesty," said the farmer, "I found this solid gold mortar in my vineyard and thought that the only place to display it was your palace. I would like you to have it." The king picked up the mortar and admired it. Then he asked, "Where is the pestle?"

The farmer slapped his brow and exclaimed, "She guessed it— word for word." The king asked, "Who guessed what?" The farmer told him that his daughter had told him exactly what the king would say when he saw the gift. The king observed that his daughter must be a very clever girl. He decided to find out how clever she was. He gave the farmer some flax to take to his daughter to make shirts for an entire regiment of soldiers. He said to tell her to make them quickly because they were needed without delay.

The farmer was shocked, but he knew better than to argue with the king. He picked up the bundle, which contained only a few strands of flax, bowed to the king, and left for home without receiving any thanks for the golden mortar.

When the farmer reached home, he relayed the king's request and told Catherine that she was in a lot of trouble. She told her father that he was upset needlessly. She took the bundle of flax and shook it. She reminded her father that there were always scalings in flax, even if it had been carded by an expert to disentangle the fibers and raise the nap prior to spinning.

A few scalings fell on the floor; Catherine picked them up and handed them to her father. She told him to return to the king and tell him that she agreed to make the shirts. However, since she had no loom to weave the cloth she said to tell the king to have one made out these scalings. Because he was king, his order would be carried out without question.

The farmer was afraid to go back to palace, but Catherine insisted, and reluctantly the farmer repeated her request to the king. Having learned how cunning Catherine was, the king was determined to meet her. He asked the farmer to tell Catherine to come to the palace so he could talk with her.

The king ordered Catherine to come to him neither clothed nor naked, on neither a full nor an empty stomach, neither during the daytime nor at night, and neither on foot nor on horseback. He told the farmer that she must follow his directions without exception or both he and his daughter would be in serious trouble. The farmer returned home in a dejected state. Catherine told him not to worry; everything was going to work out. She asked her father to bring her a fishing net.

In the morning, Catherine draped herself in the fishing net (she was neither clothed nor naked), ate some seeds from the lupine plant (her stomach was neither empty nor full), led out the nanny goat and straddled it, with one foot dragging on the ground and one foot in the air (she was neither on foot nor on horseback), and reached the palace just as the sky grew lighter, neither day nor night.

The palace guards thought Catherine was a mad woman, dressed as she was. When she told them that she was just following the orders of the king, they escorted her to the royal chambers. She announced to the king that she was here in compliance with his orders. He laughed until his sides hurt.

The king called her clever Catherine and told her that she was just the girl he was looking for. He told her that he would marry her and make her his queen on one condition: she must never pry into his business. He feared that she was smarter than he was.

When Catherine's father heard about it, he told her that she had no choice but to marry the king. However, he told her to be careful, because the king made abrupt decisions. What he decides he wanted one day, he might not want the next. The farmer told her that he would leave her work clothes hanging on a hook. If she ever had to come home, she would find them ready to put back on.

Catherine was so happy that she didn't even listen to her father. The wedding was celebrated a few days later. Festivities were held throughout the kingdom, including a large fair in the capital. Inns were filled to capacity; many farmers slept in the town squares, which were crowded all the way to the king's palace.

One farmer brought a pregnant cow to the fair to sell. He could find no shelter for the cow, so an innkeeper told him he could put it under a shed at the inn and tie it to another farmer's cart. That night, the cow gave birth. The next morning the owner of the cow was leading the cow and newborn calf away, when the owner of the cart stopped him. He told the cow's owner that he could take the cow, but that the calf was his.

The owner of the cow protested, pointing out that he owned the mother of the calf. The second farmer claimed ownership of the calf, because he owned the cart and the cow had given birth while tied to the cart. A heated quarrel ensued and before long they were fighting. A large crowd gathered, and, eventually, two constables came and separated the men. The constables took the two farmers to the king's court of justice.

According to custom, the queen was also asked for her opinion about the rulings of the court. Unfortunately, every time the king delivered a judgment, Catherine opposed it. The king grew weary of this and reminded Catherine he had asked her not to meddle in his business. He ordered her to stay out of the hall of justice, and she did. From then on, farmers went before the king alone.

In the case before the court, the king sided with the owner of the cart. The owner of the cow considered the decision unjust. Since the king's judgment was final, however, he could do nothing further. Nevertheless, the innkeeper suggested that the owner of the cow approach the queen, who might be able to find a solution to his problem. The farmer went to the palace and was told he could not see the queen, and that the king had forbidden her to hear the people's cases.

The farmer walked over to the garden wall and could see the queen on the other side. He jumped over the wall, presented his case, and told her how unjust her husband had been to him. Catherine told him the king was going hunting the next day near a lake that was always dried up this time of year. She advised the farmer to take a fishing rod with him and pretend to be fishing in the lake when the king passed by. He would laugh and ask why someone would fish in a dry lake. She advised the farmer to tell him, "Your majesty, if a cart can give birth to a calf, maybe I can catch a fish in a dry lake."

The next morning, the farmer sat on the shore of the dry lake with his fishing line resting on soil of the bottom. The king approached him, laughed, and asked him if he was out of his mind. The farmer answered just as he had been instructed. The king observed that someone else had been involved in this and asked the farmer if he had been talking to the queen. The farmer didn't deny it. The king reversed his judgment and awarded the calf to him.

When he returned to the palace, the king sent for Catherine and observed that she had been meddling in his affairs again, the very thing he had told her she could not do. He told her to return to her father and be a farm girl once again but to take with her the thing that she liked most in the palace. She asked if she could wait until the next morning to leave; otherwise people would gossip. The king agreed to dine with her that evening, but insisted that she must leave the next day.

Sly Catherine asked the cooks to prepare roasts, hams, and other heavy food to make the king drowsy and thirsty. Then she had the best wines brought up from the cellar. The king gorged himself while Catherine emptied several bottles of wine into his seemingly bottomless glass. He became drowsy. His eyes glazed over; he stopped talking and fell into a sound sleep in his great chair. Catherine asked the servants to lift the armchair and its contents and to follow her quietly. They left the palace, passed through the city gate, and didn't stop until she reached her house late in the evening.

Catherine pounded on the door and asked her father to open up. He called out to her, reminding her that he had said she would be back. He told her it was good that he had left her work clothes hanging on the hook. He opened the door and saw the servants carrying the king's chair with him in it. She had the king carried into her room, where the servants placed the king on her bed. She dismissed the servants, undressed, and lay down beside the king.

The king woke up about midnight and noticed that the mattress seemed harder than usual and the sheets rougher. He turned over and noticed Catherine beside him. He asked, "Catherine, didn't I tell you to go home?" She told him that it wasn't daylight yet and to go back to sleep. He did as he was told and woke up in the morning to the braying of a donkey and the bleating of sheep. He saw the sun streaming through the window and realized that he was not in the royal bedchamber. He turned to his wife and asked where they were.

Catherine answered, "Didn't you tell me, majesty, to return home with the thing I liked best of all? I took you, and I'm keeping you." The king laughed, and they made up. They returned to the royal palace, where they still live. From that day on, the king never appeared in the hall of justice without his wife.

Moral: On occasion, those around you have better judgment than you. Two or more heads are usually better than one, if only to use as sounding boards.

Based on: Italo Calvino, "Catherine, Sly Country Lass," *Italian Folk Tales*

Lose Your Temper and Lose Your Bet

A poor man had three sons: Giovanni, Fiore, and Pirolo. He became ill and called his sons to his bedside. They could see that he wasn't well, and he admitted that he was dying. He told them that all he had to leave to them was equal shares of the money earned by his hard work. He had time only to tell each son to take one third and manage it to the best of his ability, when he gasped his last breath and died.

The sons took their bags of money, but the oldest son, Giovanni, reminded his brothers that it would not last forever, and that they would be out in the cold when it was gone. He suggested that one of them look for work. The middle son, Fiore, agreed with his older brother and offered to go out into the world and see if he could find a job. He rose early the next morning, put on his best clothes, took his bag of money, hugged his brothers, and set out.

Fiore spent the entire day looking for work and, early in the evening, passed a church and saw a priest outside getting some fresh air. The priest, whose name was Don Raimondo, asked where Fiore was going. He told the priest that he was going into the world seeking his fortune. Don Raimondo asked Fiore what he had in the bag and was told that it was his share of money left by his father. The priest invited him into his household and told him that he had a share of money too.

Don Raimondo invited Fiore to enter his service on one condition: that the first one to lose his temper would also lose his share of money. Fiore accepted the priest's terms and was shown a plot of land to be tilled the next day. The priest promised to have breakfast and dinner brought to Fiore in the field, saving him trips back to the house. Fiore agreed with this arrangement over supper that evening, after the older of two servant women showed him to his room.

Fiore got up early the next morning and went out to till the field that the priest had shown him. He dug until breakfast time, then stopped and waited for someone to bring his breakfast. When no one came, Fiore became angry and swore. Nevertheless, he resumed tilling on an empty stomach and looked forward to dinner. Fiore worked until dinner time and looked down the road to see if anyone was bringing his dinner. With anticipation, he watched everyone that passed, but no one brought food.

At last, at dusk, one of the servant women came out to the field with many excuses, including that she had been too busy doing the laundry to bring his meals to him. In his anger, he wanted to call her every bad name he could think of; however, he did not want to forfeit his money to the priest. He reached into the woman's basket and lifted out a pot and a bottle. He attempted to take the lid off of the pot, but it appeared to be cemented on. He screamed insults at her and sent the pot flying. The woman explained that the lid was placed tightly on the pot to keep out the flies.

Next, Fiore grabbed the bottle and found that it had been sealed the same way. He screamed at the top of his lungs and told the servant to go back and tell the priest that he would hear directly that that was is no way to treat a worker. The servant returned to the house to find the priest waiting in the doorway. He asked her how it went. She replied that it had gone perfectly, and that Fiore was beside himself with rage.

A little later, Fiore returned to the house and lashed out angrily at Don Raimondo, calling him every name he could think of. The priest asked him if he had forgotten their agreement that the first one to lose his temper would forfeit his money. Fiore said that the devil could take the money, as he packed up and stomped off. The priest and his servant could not stop laughing at Fiore's misfortune.

Hungry, tired, and angry, Fiore walked home. When he arrived, his brothers could tell from the expression on his face that things had not gone well. As he ate his meal, he told them what had happened. Giovanni asked for directions to the priest's house. He said that he would go there and return not only with his own money but the priest's and Fiore's money as well.

The next day, Giovanni encountered the same treatment that his younger brother had experienced. He held out longer than Fiore, but eventually he became so enraged due to hunger and thirst that he would have forfeited ten bags of money instead of one. He returned home starving and incensed.

Pirolo, who although the youngest was the most cunning of the three, told his brothers that he would go next and would win back their money and every penny the priest had. The older brothers were reluctant to let him go; they feared the loss of all of their father's money. Finally, however, they gave in and let him go.

Pirolo arrived at Don Raimondo's house and agreed to work for him. The usual agreement was made, and the priest told him that he had three bags of money to stake against his one bag. When he sat down to supper with the priest and the two servant women, Pirolo stuffed as much bread, meat, and cheese as he could into his pockets.

Pirolo was at work in the fields before sunrise. As expected, no one showed up with his breakfast, so he took some bread and cheese out of his pocket and ate. Then, he visited a nearby farmhouse, introduced himself as the priest's field hand, and asked for something to drink. The farmer and his wife fussed over him and asked how the priest was. After chatting for a while, the farmer went to his wine cellar and drew a bowl of their fine wine for Pirolo.

Pirolo thanked the farmer and his wife, promised to call on them again, and returned to work in the fields in good spirits. As before, no one showed up with his dinner, so he finished the bread and meat in his pockets. He went back to the farmer's house again for more wine and returned to the fields singing. At dusk, one of the servants showed up with his dinner and apologized for being late. She was surprised to hear Pirolo singing. He told her being late was no problem, and that it was never too late to eat.

The servant took the pot with the sealed lid out of her carrying bag. Pirolo commented on how clever they were to fix the lid so the flies couldn't get in. He pried the lid off with his hoe and ate the soup. Then he picked up the bottle, broke off the neck with his hoe, and drank the wine. He told the woman to return to the house, and that he had some work to complete in the fields. He asked her to thank the priest for his thoughtfulness.

The priest greeted the servant on her return and asked how things had gone at the fields. She replied that she had bad news; the boy was as happy as he could be. The priest told her to wait, and that his worker would change his tune. When Pirolo returned, he sat down to supper with the priest and his servants and joked with them. Pirolo asked what work was planned for the next day. He was told that he was to take one hundred pigs to market, including one large sow, to be sold to the first merchant that he met.

Pirolo did not sell the sow. Before selling the others, he cut off their tails and brought them back with him. With the money from selling the pigs in his pocket, he headed back to the priest's house.

Along the way, he stopped at a field, dug holes with a trowel, and buried ninety-nine pigtails, leaving only the curl of each tail above ground. Next, he dug a large hole and buried the sow, leaving only her tail showing. Then he shouted as loud as he could, "Hurry, hurry, Don Raimondo; the pigs you own are going to the inferno!"

The priest looked out of the window to see what was going on, and Pirolo motioned for him to come outside. The priest ran over to where Pirolo was standing. Pirolo said that he had bad luck. He explained how he was with the herd when he saw them going under, in front of his eyes. He observed that the pigs all disappeared except for their tails, and said they must be be going down to hell. He suggested they try to save at least some of them. The priest pulled up a few but wound up with only the tails in his hand.

Pirolo went over and grabbed the sow's tail and tugged and pulled until he brought her out of the ground alive but unhappy and squealing loudly. The priest was tempted to jump up and down in anger, but he remembered their agreement. He asked what more could they do and resigned himself to accepting it. He admitted that accidents will happen and walked back to the house wringing his hands.

That evening Pirolo asked the priest what work he had for him the next day. The priest said that he had one hundred sheep to go to market but he hoped that the same thing that happened to the pigs would not happen to the sheep. Pirolo exclaimed that they could never be that unlucky again.

The next day Pirolo went to the market and sold the sheep, except for one that limped, pocketed the money, and headed home. When he reached the field where he had buried the pigtails, he picked up a ladder and leaned it against a large tree. He carried the lame sheep to the top of the tree and tied her up. Then he came down, placed the ladder back on the ground, and shouted as loudly as he could, "Hurry, hurry. Don Raimondo! The lambs you own are headed for the rainbow!"

The priest ran towards Pirolo, who explained that he was walking with the sheep when suddenly they leapt into the air as if summoned to paradise. Only the crippled one in the treetop over there didn't make it. The priest turned red with rage but maintained his composure. He admitted that nothing could be done, and that they would have to accept it.

After supper, Pirolo asked what his work for the next day would be. The priest said that he had no more tasks for him. However, the next morning he was going to say Mass in a neighboring village and asked Pirolo to come with him and to serve at the Mass.

The next morning, Pirolo woke up early, washed his face, put on a clean shirt, shined the priest's shoes, and woke up his employer. As soon as they had left the house, it started to rain. The priest asked Pirolo to return to the house for his wooden shoes because he didn't want to get his good shoes wet. The priest told him that he would wait under the nearby tree with the umbrella.

Pirolo ran into the house and told the servants that the priest had asked him to give each of them a kiss. They were astounded, and said that they could not imagine the priest saying such a thing. Pirolo said that, nevertheless, it was true, and he would verify it for them. He called out the window to the priest and asked, "One, father, or two?" The priest responded, "Why, both of them, of course! Both of them!" Pirolo gave both servants a kiss, picked up the wooden shoes, and ran back to the priest, who asked what good one shoe would have done him.

When the priest returned home, he asked the sulking servants what was bothering them. They replied that he must know what was bothering them; they could not believe that he would give the boy such instructions. The priest said that was the last straw, and he must dismiss Pirolo at once. They reminded him that he couldn't send field hands away until the cuckoo had sung. He said they would just have to pretend that the cuckoo was singing. He called Pirolo over, told him he had no more work for him, and wished him well.

Pirolo reminded the priest that he could not dismiss him until the cuckoo had sung. The priest agreed that, to be fair, they would wait for the cuckoo to sing. The older servant woman had killed and plucked feathers from several hens and sewed them onto an old waistcoat and a pair of breeches belonging to the priest. She dressed up in this outfit and climbed onto the roof during the evening. She sang, "Cuckoo! Cuckoo!"

They were eating supper when the priest said that he could hear the cuckoo singing. Pirolo said that it couldn't be the cuckoo because it was early March, and the cuckoo never sang until May.

Nevertheless, both could hear the cuckoo singing. Pirolo ran to get the shotgun from the wall behind the priest's bed, opened the window, and aimed at the large bird on the roof. The priest begged him not to shoot, but he fired the gun anyway. The feather-clad servant tumbled off the roof, riddled with buckshot.

The priest growled with rage, told Pirolo to get out, and that he never wanted to see him again. Pirolo asked him if he was angry, and the priest admitted that he certainly was. Pirolo went home with four bags of money, as well as the proceeds from the sale of the pigs and the sheep. He returned his brothers' shares to them and opened a clothing store with his share. He married and lived happily ever after.

Moral: When you are taken advantage of, beat those who have taken advantage of you at their own game without losing your temper. Turnabout, not revenge, is fair play.

Based on: Italo Calvino, "Lose Your Temper, and You Lose Your Bet," *Italian Folktales*

Honesty and Dishonesty

One day, two Russian peasants were passing the time talking. One was boastful and untruthful; the other was known for his honesty. The first peasant said that it was better to tell lies, cheat everybody, and be rich. The second peasant replied that it was better to live in poverty as long as you were truthful. They quarreled; neither was willing to give in. They decided to walk along the road that went through the village and ask the first person they met.

They saw a peasant plowing a field adjacent to the road and asked his opinion to resolve their dispute. They asked him if it was better to live in the world by telling the truth or by telling lies. He told them that it was not possible to live honestly in the world for a lifetime; that everyone must lie occasionally. Besides, an honest man must walk about all his life in cheap shoes, whereas a dishonest man can walk in expensive boots.

From his place behind the plow, the peasant pointed out that their masters gave them no days off. To get a day off from work, they had to say that they are sick. Also, if they wanted to cut firewood in the forest, they had to do it at night, because cutting wood is forbidden during the day. He concluded that people must be sneaky in this world in order to survive. The first peasant said to the second peasant, "See, I told you so."

The truthful peasant was not convinced. They walked down the road and encountered a merchant driving a wagon. They asked him the same question: whether it was better to live honestly in the world or dishonestly. The merchant observed how difficult it was to live honestly. He said it was better to be dishonest. Furthermore, he added, people cheat us, so why should we not cheat them? The first peasant pointed out that here was another person who agreed with him. The second peasant was still not persuaded.

Farther down the road, they met a nobleman whom they asked the same question. The nobleman said that being dishonest was the only way to get on in the world. He asked what honesty and truthfulness there was in the world. He noted that if you were honest and told the truth, you got sent to Siberia.

The dishonest peasant told the honest peasant that everyone agreed with him; it was better to live dishonestly. The truthful man still disagreed. He said that it was not better, and he did not intend to live that way. He said that if misfortunes happened to him because of this, he would let them happen.

The peasants traveled together for a while, looking for work. The dishonest man adapted himself to the company he was in; wherever he went he ate well, drank well, and did not have to pay. The honest man had to pay for every drop of water and morsel of bread he got; nevertheless, he did not grumble. He was perfectly satisfied. The dishonest man laughed inwardly as he watched his traveling companion.

Eventually, they passed the last village and were in open country with no houses or inns. The honest man grew very hungry and asked his companion for a morsel of bread, knowing that he had plenty. His companion asked him what he would give him for the bread. The honest peasant told him to take anything he liked, although he did not have much to give. The dishonest man then asked to let him put out his eye. Surprisingly, the starving man agreed, and he received a small piece of bread in return for the loss of an eye.

They continued down the road until the honest man became

extremely hungry again and asked for another piece of bread. His companion agreed to give him another piece of bread if he could knock out his other eye. The honest man said, "If you do that, brother, I shall be blind." However, the honest man could not tolerate hunger. So he told his companion that, if he was not afraid of committing the sin, he could put out his other eye.

The dishonest man did the evil deed and gave his companion an even smaller piece of bread than the first time. Then he left his companion in the middle of the deserted countryside. He told his blind companion that he would have to find his way by himself; he was not going to lead a blind man around. The blind man finished his morsel of bread and tried to feel his way along the road. He hoped that he might find the next village.

Soon, he lost his way and did not know where to go. He stopped, dropped to his knees, and began to pray. He asked the saints not to forsake him, though he was a sinner. He prayed for a long time. Finally, he heard a voice that told him: "Turn to your right, good man, and you will come to a forest where you will hear the murmur of a fountain; feel your way to it, bathe your eyes in the clear water, and your eyesight will be restored. You will see a large oak tree; climb up into it, and stop there for the night.

The blind man turned to the right and finally reached the forest with some difficulty. He crawled along a path that led to the murmuring fountain, dipped his hands into the water, and bathed his eyes. His eyesight returned immediately, and he looked around with awe and gratitude. The oak tree was near the fountain. The grass under the tree seemed to have been trampled and the earth around it dug up and scattered. He climbed the tree and waited for nightfall.

About midnight, many evil spirits came to the base of the tree and began to boast about where they had been and what they had done. One little devil bragged, "I went to the beautiful princess, the king's daughter, and tormented her all day. I have tormented her for over ten years, and no one can cast me out. Many a handsome prince has tried, but all in vain; no one will ever succeed unless he obtains that large, famous image of the Virgin Mary that is owned by a wealthy merchant. No one will ever think of that, and, if they do, the merchant will never part with it."

In the morning, all the devils had left, and the truthful man climbed down from the tree and went in search of the wealthy merchant. After inquiring around, the honest man found the merchant. He offered to work for him for a year without wages, if he would give him the large image of the Virgin Mary as payment.

The merchant agreed, and the man, anxious to satisfy his master, worked hard day and night. After a year, he came to his master and asked for his reward. The rich merchant told him that he was satisfied with his work, but he was reluctant to give up the famous image. He asked his worker to take money instead. The conscientious worker said that money would be of no use to him, and that he wanted what had been promised to him a year ago.

The wealthy man told the truthful man that if he would work for him another year without wages, he would give up the image of the Virgin Mary. The honest man had no alternative, so he agreed to work another year without wages. At the end of the year, the rich man again refused to part with the image. The honest man was very disappointed; however, the merchant was influential, and it did not seem wise to take him on under the circumstances. So the honest man agreed, reluctantly, to work another year without pay.

The truthful man worked even harder the third year than he had the first two years. At the end of the third year, the merchant took the image down from the wall and gave it to his worker, saying: "Take it, my good fellow, for you have worked so hard and so well, without ever grumbling, that I cannot refuse you this time. Take it, and may the saints bless you."

The truthful man thanked the merchant and took the image to the king's palace, where the little devil was tormenting the princess. He told the servants and courtiers that he could cure the princess. He was brought before the king, who was sitting on his throne looking miserable. The king took him to the quarters of the princess. The honest man asked for a large bowl of fresh water, dipped the picture in it three times, and brought the water to the beautiful princess. He instructed her to bathe her face in it. Immediately, the demon sprang out of he water, writhing in agony until he became lifeless. When the devil had expired, the lovely young woman became happy and radiant again.

The king and queen were overjoyed and did not know how to reward the man who had been such an excellent doctor. They wanted to make him a noble or to give him many treasures; he refused all of it and told them that he did not want anything. The princess told the king that she would marry the young man, if he would have her. The king agreed, and the young man certainly did not object.

The wedding feast was prepared, and news of the impending marriage spread around the kingdom far and wide. A huge crowd gathered to see the bride and bridegroom on their wedding day. From that day onward, the truthful man lived in the palace, dressed in royal garments, and dined at the king's table.

Time passed, and the honest man told the king and queen that he would like to travel to his own country. His mother was old and still lived in his village; he wanted to return to visit her. The princess offered to accompany him. They rode in a royal carriage. Along their route, they encountered the wretch who had put out his eyes. The king's son-in-law stopped the carriage and asked the man how he was. He then asked whether he remembered the man he had quarreled with about honesty and dishonesty and whose eyes he had knocked out.

The wretch trembled. He did not know what to say or do. The king's son-in-law told him not to worry; he was not angry and planned no retribution. He explained everything to the dishonest man: how he had gone to the forest, what he had heard there, how he had worked for three years, received the image of the Virgin Mary, and married the king's daughter.

After hearing this, the dishonest man decided to go into forest and climb up the old oak tree himself. He hoped to be as fortunate and his companion had been. He found the fountain and the oak tree, which he climbed. There he waited until nightfall. At midnight, the evil spirits came from all directions to the grass beneath the tree. Unfortunately, this time the spirits looked up and saw the dishonest man hiding in the tree. They hauled him down, gave him a lantern and an endless supply of candles, and ordered him to walk around, like Diogenes looking for a honest man, from then until eternity.

Moral: Honesty is the best policy.

Based on: Edith M. S. Hodgetts, "Honesty and Dishonesty," *Tales and Legends from the Land of the Tzar*

The Choice of Hercules

Hercules, a hero of classical mythology noted for great strength, was young and his life was all before him when he went out one morning. As he walked, however, his heart was filled with bitterness when he looked around and saw others who were living lives of ease and pleasure. He was envious, because he was experiencing only the labor and pain of obligations. As he thought about his life in comparison with others, he approached a fork in the road and was unsure which road to take. The road on the right was hilly and rough. He could see no beauty along it, but he saw that it led directly to the majestic blue mountains in the far distance.

The road to the left was wide and smooth, with beautiful trees on each side containing birds singing sweetly and surrounded by flowers. Unfortunately, it ended in fog before it reached the blue mountains that attracted him in the distance.

While Hercules stood at the fork in the road, he saw two fair young women coming towards him, one on the left road, the other on the right. The one on the flowery road reached him first; he saw that she was as beautiful as a summer day. Her cheeks were red, her eyes sparkled, and she spoke warmly and persuasively.

She said, "Oh noble youth, be no longer bowed down with labor and sore trials, but come and follow me. I will lead you into pleasant paths, where there are no storms to disturb and no troubles to annoy. You shall live in ease, with one unending round of music and mirth; you shall not want for anything that makes life joyous — sparkling wine, or soft couches, or rich robes, or the loving eyes of beautiful maidens. Come with me, and life shall be to you a daydream of gladness."

By this time, the other fair woman had also approached Hercules. She said, "I have nothing to promise you but that which you win with your own strength. The road upon which I would lead you is uneven and hard. It climbs many a hill and descends into many a valley and quagmire. The views that you will sometimes get from the hilltops are grand and glorious, but the deep valleys are dark, and the ascent from them is toilsome. Nevertheless, the road leads to the blue mountains of endless fame, which you see far away on the horizon. They cannot be reached without labor; in fact, nothing is worth having if not won by toil. If you would have fruits and flowers, you must plant them and care for them; if you would gain the love of your fellow men, you must love them and suffer for them; if you would enjoy the favor of heaven, you must make yourself worthy of that favor; if you would have eternal fame, you must not scorn the hard road that leads to it."

Hercules observed that this young woman, although as beautiful as the other, had a face that was pure and gentle, like the sky on a balmy May morning. He asked what her name was. She replied, "Some call me Labor, but others know me as Virtue."

Hercules turned to the first young woman and asked her what her name was. She said, with a bewitching smile, "Some call me Pleasure, but I prefer to be known as the Joyous and Happy One."

Hercules said, "Virtue, I will take you as my guide! The road of labor and honest effort shall be mine, and my heart shall no longer harbor bitterness or discontent." He placed his hand into the hand of Virtue, and walked with her up the hilly and forbidding road that led to the majestic blue mountains on the horizon.

Hercules was known for accomplishing his twelve labors, which included cleaning the accumulation of thirty years in the vast Augean stables, conquering the Amazons, and bringing up Cerberus from the lower world.

Moral: Achievement must be earned by hard work.

Based on: James Baldwin, "The Choice of Hercules,"
Fifty Famous Stories Retold

Chapter 4

PERSEVERING / RESOURCEFUL

Nothing in the world can take the place of persistence.
Talent will not; nothing is more common than
    unsuccessful men with talent.
Genius will not; unrewarded genius is almost a proverb.
Education alone will not; the world is full of educated derelicts.
Persistence and determination alone are omnipotent.

                         Anonymous

Robert Bruce: The Tale of the Spider

In 1305 and early 1306, Scotland was ruled by Edward I of England, a strong, cruel Plantagenet king. Scotland had been a conquered country, or at least partly under English rule, since 1296. The Scottish patriot, William Wallace, had tried to throw off the English yoke with a rousing victory at Stirling Bridge in September 1297, but his forces lost the battle of Falkirk to the English longbow the following July and were reduced to guerrilla actions. Wallace was a commoner with no aspirations to the crown of Scotland.

In 1306, the two Scottish lords with the greatest claim to the throne were John Comyn of Badenoch, "the Red Comyn," nephew of the previous king, John Balliol, and Robert Bruce, whose grandfather had been King of Scotland. John Comyn had been in communication with Edward I of England. When Robert Bruce heard of these discussions, he suggested that Comyn meet with him in the Church of the Minorite Friars in Dumfries.

The heirs to the throne argued heatedly near the high altar, and Robert Bruce fatally stabbed the Red Comyn. Bruce's companions claimed that it was self-defense. Bruce was concerned about losing the support of the church by this act but was pardoned by the patriotic Bishop of Glasgow, Bishop Wishart. On Palm Sunday, 1306, Bruce was crowned Robert I, King of Scotland, at Scone.

Scotland was a divided country, and many Scottish lords sided with the English. Bruce's early encounters with the English and their Scottish allies were a series of defeats. In June 1306, he was routed at the battle of Methven in his first battle as King of Scotland. During the battle, Bruce was taken prisoner briefly but was rescued by his brother-in-law, Christopher Seton. Bishop Wishart was captured and imprisoned. Six of the knights who had supported Bruce at his coronation were captured, and sixteen nobles, including Christopher Seton, were hanged at Newcastle without a trial.

Bruce's rule was at an ebb, and many of his supporters were discouraged. He attempted to enlist men for his small army at Athol. In August 1306, Bruce and his party camped on land belonging to John of Lorne, a distant Comyn relative, who had heard that Bruce was in the area and had asked his tenants to watch for him and his men. Bruce's party was surprised by John of Lorne's men, and the King of Scotland was defeated again. Many of Bruce's party dispersed to avoid capture.

With a small following, Bruce "took to the heather," sleeping in caves and eating only drammock, a mixture of raw oatmeal and water. After crossing Loch Lomond to Castle Donaverty, Bruce and his men traveled among the Islands of Kintyre and the Hebrides, participating in several forays and skirmishes along the way. Bruce and his men wintered on the Island of Rathlin off the coast of Ireland. The Irish natives didn't provide aid to the refugee Scots but, because they were hostile to the English, didn't betray them to King Edward's forces.

According to a tale passed down from generation to generation, the incident of the spider occurred at Rathlin. Bruce thought his problems might be due to his killing the Red Comyn in the church at Dumfries, and he considered performing an act of contrition for this great sin. He thought about abandoning his quest to free Scotland from English rule to go on a crusade to the Holy Land against the Saracens. Still, he didn't want to shirk his duty as King of Scotland to free his country from the English invaders. He was torn between performing his duty to Scotland and atoning for past sins. According to Sir Walter Scott in "History of Scotland" from *Tales of a Grandfather:*

> While he was divided twixt these reflections, and doubtful of what he would do, Bruce was looking upward toward the roof of the cabin in which he lay; and his eye was attracted by a spider which, hanging at the end of a long thread of its own spinning, was endeavoring, in the fashion of that creature, to swing itself from one beam in the roof to another, for the purpose of fixing the line on which it meant to stretch its web. The insect made the attempt again and again without success, and at length Bruce counted that it had tried to carry its point six times, and been as often unable to do so. It came to his head that he had himself fought just six battles against the English and their allies, and that the poor persevering spider was exactly in the same situation as himself, having made as many trials, and had been as often disappointed in what he had aimed at.

"Now," thought Bruce, "as I have no means of knowing what is best to be done, I shall be guided by the luck that guides this spider. If the spider shall make another effort to fix its thread and shall be successful, I will venture a seventh time to try my fortune in Scotland; but if the spider shall fail, I will go to the wars in Palestine, and never return to my home country more." While Bruce was forming his resolution, the spider made another exertion with all the force it could muster, and fairly succeeded in fastening its thread to the beam which it had so often in vain attempted to reach. Bruce, seeing the success of the spider, resolved to try his own fortune; and as he had never before gained a victory, so he never afterward sustained any considerable or decisive check or defeat.

Bruce defeated the English decisively at Bannockburn in June 1314 and finally, in 1328, achieved his goal: formal recognition of the independence of Scotland by the English Parliament.

Moral: At a speech at the Harrow School on October 29, 1941, Prime Minister Winston Churchill said: "Never give in, never give in, never, never, never, never—except to convictions of honor and good sense."

Based on: Sir Walter Scott, "History of Scotland," *Tales of a Grandfather*

The Blemish on the Diamond

A king once owned a magnificent diamond of the highest quality. He was very proud to possess it; it had no equal in the world. Even though diamonds are composed of pure carbon and are one of the hardest substances known to man, they can be damaged. One day, an accident occurred and the diamond was deeply scratched. The king was beside himself. He consulted with several diamond cutters, the most highly regarded artists in their speciality. They all told him that no matter what they did or how much they ground and polished the stone, they could not completely remove the imperfection.

Months later, at the request of the king, the most highly regarded lapidary in the country visited the capital and began work to make the diamond even more beautiful and more valuable than before the accident. With the greatest artistry, he engraved a delicate rosebud around the imperfection and used the scratch as the stem. It was an ingenious solution to the problem. When the king and the other diamond cutters who had seen the diamond in its flawed condition saw it, they were filled with admiration of the workmanship.

Moral: With perseverance, we can transform our worst
shortcomings into virtues. We should not be restricted by
conventional solutions to a problem.

Based on: Nathan Ausubel, "The Blemish on the Diamond,"
A Treasury of Jewish Folklore

The Perseverance of Job

Job was a good man who lived thousands of years ago, in the time of Moses or later. He lived on the edge of the desert, east of the land of Israel, and had seven sons and three daughters. He was a very rich man who owned 500 asses, 3,000 camels, 500 yoke of oxen, and 7,000 sheep. No man in all of the East was as rich as Job.

Job prayed and served the Lord every day. He was kind and gentle, made offerings upon God's altar and tried to live as God wished him to live. He treated his fellow man as he wished to be treated. Every day, when his sons were working in the field or when they were feasting together, Job went to his altar to make a burnt offering for each of his sons and daughters and prayed for them. He said, "It may be that my sons have sinned or have turned away from God in their hearts; I will pray to God to forgive them."

One time when the angels of God stood before the Lord, Satan came also and stood among them, as though he were one of God's angels. When the Lord saw Satan, He asked, "Satan, from what place have you come?" Satan replied, "I have come from going up and down the earth and looking at the people in it."

The Lord asked Satan, "Have you looked at my servant Job?

Have you seen there is not another such man on earth, a perfect man, one who fears God and does nothing evil?" Satan asked the Lord, "Does Job fear God for nothing? Have You not made a wall around him, around his house, and around everything that he has? You have given a blessing upon his work, and have made him rich. But if You will stretch forth Your hand, and take away from him all that he has, then he will turn away from You and will curse You to Your face."

The Lord responded to the fallen angel, "Satan, all that Job has is in your power; you can do to his sons, his flocks of sheep, his cattle, whatever you wish; only lay not your hand on the man himself."

Satan sallied forth from the Lord; soon trouble visited Job. One day, when Job's sons and daughters were dining in the oldest brother's house, a man came running to Job and told him: "The oxen were behind the plows, and the asses were feeding alongside them, when wild Sabeans from the desert attacked and drove them all away. The men who were plowing with the oxen and caring for the asses have all been killed with the sword. I am the only one who has escaped!"

Before the first man had finished speaking, another man rushed up to Job and told him: "Lightning from the sky has struck all of the sheep and shepherds; I am the only one who has survived." Before he had finished, a third man approached Job and said: "Three bands of our enemies from Chaldea have come and taken all of the camels. They have killed all of the men who were with them except me."

A fourth man ran up to Job to tell him: "Your sons and daughters were eating and drinking together in your oldest son's house, when a sudden and devastating wind from the desert struck the house, and it fell in on them. All of your sons and daughters are dead; I alone have lived to tell you of it."

In one day, all of Job's children and possessions were taken away. He had been rich; now he was poor and without a family. Job fell down on his knees before his God and said, "With nothing I came into the world, and with nothing I shall leave it. The Lord gave, and the Lord has taken away; blessed be the name of the Lord." Even when all was taken away from Job, he did not forsake his God, nor did he question God's actions.

Again the angels of God were before Him, and Satan, who had caused Job all of this harm, was among them. The Lord asked Satan, "Have you looked at my servant Job? No other man in the world is as good as he, a perfect man, one who fears God and does no wrong. Notice how he holds fast to his goodness, even after I have let you do him such great harm?"

Satan answered, "All that a man has he will give for his life. But if You would put hand upon him and touch his bone and his flesh, he will turn from You, and will curse You to Your face." The Lord told Satan, "I will give Job into your hands. Do to him whatever you please; only spare his life."

Satan went out again and struck Job and caused painful boils all over his body, from the soles of his feet to the top of his head. Job sat down in the ashes in great pain; he did not speak one word against his God. His wife asked him, "What is the use of trying to serve God? You may as well curse him and die!" Job told her: "You speak as though you were foolish. We take good things from the Lord. Shall we not take bad things also?"

Job would not speak out against the Lord. Three of his friends came to comfort him in his misfortune and pain. Eliphaz, Bildad, and Sophar sat down with Job, wept, and commiserated with him. However, their words were not words of comfort.

They believed that all of Job's troubles had rained down on him because he had committed some great sin. They tried to persuade their friend to tell them what he had done to deserve such punishment and to make God so angry with him.

In those times, people believed that trouble, sickness, and loss occurred to men when they had made God angry because of their sins. The three friends thought that Job must have been very wicked to bring such evil down on himself. They urged him to confess his wickedness. Job told them that he had done no wrong; in fact, he had always tried to do what was right. He did not know why these troubles had come to him, but he would not say that God was unjust in causing him to suffer.

Job did not understand God's ways, but he believed that God was good; he left himself in God's hands. Finally, God spoke to Job and his friends. He told them that it is not for man to judge God, and that God will do right by every man. The Lord told the three friends of Job: "You have spoken of me what is right, as Job has.

Now bring an offering to me; Job shall pray for you, and for his sake, I forgive you."

Job prayed for his friends, and God forgave them. Because in all of his troubles, Job had remained faithful to God, the Lord blessed Job once more, took away his boils, and made him well. Then the Lord gave Job more than he ever had in the past: twice as many asses, camels, oxen, and sheep. And God gave again to Job, seven sons and three daughters. In all the land, no women were as lovely as Job's daughters. After his troubles, Job lived a long time, in goodness, honor, and wealth, under God's care.

Moral: Keep your faith even in trying times. Persevere and be patient and, hopefully, over the long term, the good will outweigh the bad.

Based on: Book of Job 42.1-31, *The Holy Bible*

The Set of Emeralds
My friend and I had stopped in front of Duran's bookstore on the Street of San Jeronimo in Madrid and were browsing the titles of the books in the window. My attention was called to some unusual titles, and I commented on them to the friend who had accompanied me. He exclaimed: "Forget those books, the day could not be more beautiful. Let's go by the Fuente Castellana. While we are walking, I will tell you a story in which I am the principal hero."

I had plenty to do; but since I am always glad for an excuse to do nothing, I went along with his suggestion. My friend began his story as follows: "One night some time ago, I set out to stroll the streets without any definite object. After having examined all the collections of prints and photographs in shop windows, I chose, in imagination in front of the Savoyard store, the bronzes with which I would adorn my house, if I had one. Also, after having made a minute survey of all the objects of art and luxury exposed to public view upon the shelves behind the lighted plate glass, I stopped for a moment at Samper's jewelry store.

"I do not know how long I remained there, adorning, in fancy, all the pretty women I knew, one with a collar of pearls, another with a cross of diamonds, another with earrings of amethyst and gold. I was deliberating at that point to whom to offer—who would be worthy of it—a magnificent set of emeralds as rich as it was elegant, which among all the other jewelled ornaments claimed attention for the beauty and clearness of its stones. Then I heard at my side the softest, sweetest voice exclaim with an accent that could not fail to put my fancies to flight: 'What beautiful emeralds!'

"I turned to see who had been impressed with the emeralds and observed an extremely beautiful woman whose loveliness made a profound impression on me. I could envision what the emeralds would look like around the attractive neck of the young woman. She left the store and entered an elegant carriage; I noted the crest on the carriage. She must be a wealthy lady of high rank. By tracing the crest, I found that the young woman had been married while still a child to a wastrel who had squandered his fortune and sought an alliance that would provide another fortune to pay for his dissipation.

"When I uncovered the facts of the situation in which the young woman found herself, I was even more strongly motivated to obtain the necklace for her. From the time that I had uncovered the mystery of her life, all of my aspirations were reduced to one—to get possession of those wonderful jewels and to give them to her in a way that she could not refuse them, nor even know from whom they came.

"Unfortunately, I had no money, but I did not despair. I wrote a book and used the proceeds to purchase the necklace. My book, *The Set of Emeralds*, was of original quality but was not popular; it earned only $150, a small fraction of the $15,000 cost of the emeralds. I decided to gamble the $150 to accumulate enough to buy the necklace.

"In order to win, one must place a bet with the full expectation of winning. If you approach the gaming tables with the hesitancy of one who merely wants to try his luck, you will lose. One should put down his money with the coolness of one who has come to claim what is owed him. Fortunately, I gambled wisely with confidence and in one night won $15,000. My confidence level was so high, I would have been surprised to lose.

"The next day I went to Samper's and bought the emeralds without a second thought about other possible uses of my recently gained windfall. My winnings could have been used for a year of pleasure, many beautiful women, a vacation in Italy, and as many cigars and glasses of champagne as I desired. Nevertheless, I did not waver.

"My next task was to find a way to deliver the necklace to the object of my admiration. I realized it could not be a outright gift from a stranger. I arranged for one of the lady's maids, for several hundred dollars, to place the necklace in milady's jewel box and then move to Barcelona.

"Several months passed and the young woman had not worn the necklace in public; nevertheless, she had made a great effort to determine, without success, the source of the emeralds. One evening, I stationed myself at the entrance to the palace prior to a royal ball to await her carriage. She created a stir when she stepped from her carriage and entered the palace wearing the necklace and looking radiant. I could not prevent myself from uttering a low, involuntary cry. The women looked at her with envy; the men stared at her with admiration and longing. My efforts had been worthwhile."

Moral: It is better to give than to receive. Much satisfaction is gained by placing others in a higher priority than yourself.

Based on: Gustavo Adolpho Becquer, "The Set of Emeralds," *Romantic Legends of Spain*

Intelligence and Luck

Once upon a time, Luck met Intelligence sitting on a bench in a garden. Luck asked Intelligence to make room for him. Intelligence was inexperienced and wasn't sure who should make room for whom. Intelligence asked why he should make room for Luck since Luck was no better than he. Luck answered that the better man is the one who performs most. Luck pointed at the peasant's son plowing in the nearby field and challenged Intelligence to enter into the plowboy's head to see if he gets on better through him or through Luck.

As soon as the young peasant, Vanek, began to think that he had Intelligence in his head, he questioned why he should have to be behind the plow for the rest of his life. He went home and told

65

his father that he wanted to be a gardener. His father asked what ailed him, and if he had lost his wits. Nevertheless, he said that if that is what his oldest son wanted to do, he should be allowed to try. He told Vanek that his younger brother would inherit the family farm instead of him

Vanek became an apprentice to the king's gardener. Soon, he began to comprehend more about gardening than the gardener was able to teach him. He no longer followed the gardener's instructions; he did things his own way. Initially, the gardener was angry, but, when he saw that everything was growing better, he stopped complaining. He observed that Vanek was more intelligent than he, and he let Vanek do as he pleased.

The garden became so beautiful that the king thoroughly enjoyed it and frequently took long walks in it with the queen and his only daughter. The princess was a beautiful young woman who, when she was twelve years old, had stopped speaking. The king grieved that no one heard a word from her. He issued a proclamation that anyone who could encourage her to speak again would be welcomed as her husband.

Many young kings, princes, and other great lords came and went, unsuccessful in encouraging her to speak. Vanek decided to see what he could do. He thought that if he could ask a question in the right way, it might motivate the princess to speak. He announced himself at the palace. The king and his counselors accompanied Vanek to his daughter's sitting room. The princess had a friendly little dog of whom she was very fond because he was so clever and seemed to understand everything she wanted.

When Vanek entered the sitting room, he pretended not even to see the princess. He turned to the dog and said, "I have heard, doggie, that you are very clever, and I come to you for advice. We were three companions in travel: a sculptor, a tailor, and me. Once upon a time, we were traveling through a forest and were obliged to spend the night in it. To be safe from wolves, we made a fire and agreed to keep watch, one after the other.

"The sculptor kept watch first and, to amuse himself, took a log and carved a doll out of it. When the carving was finished, he woke the tailor to take the next watch. The tailor saw the carving and asked the sculptor why he had carved it. He replied that he was weary and didn't know what to do with himself. The sculptor told the tailor that if he found time hanging heavy on his hands, he could dress her.

"The tailor took out his scissors, needle, and thread, cut clothes out of material, and sewed them together. When he finished, he dressed the doll in the clothes and called me to keep the next watch. I asked the tailor what was going on. He explained that the sculptor had been bored so he had carved the damsel out of a log, and that he had time on his hands so he clothed her. The tailor told me if I found time hanging heavy on my hands that I could teach her to speak. I did my part, and by the time the sun came up in the morning, I had actually taught her to speak."

When my companions woke up in the morning, each wanted to possess the damsel. The sculptor said, "I made her." The tailor said, "I clothed her." I, too, claimed my rights: "Therefore, doggie, tell me to whom the doll belongs." The dog said nothing, but the princess replied instead, "To whom can she belong, but to you? What's the good of the sculptor's damsel without life? What's the good of the tailor's clothing without speech? You gave her the best gift, life and speech, and therefore, by right she belongs to you."

Vanek told her, "You have passed your own sentence. I have given you speech again and a new life, and you therefore by right belong to me."

One of the king's councilors said, "His royal highness will give you a substantial reward for succeeding in loosening his daughter's tongue, but you cannot marry her because you are of mean lineage."

The king agreed and told Vanek, "I will give you a plentiful reward instead of our daughter."

Vanek wouldn't hear of any other reward and said, "The king promised, without any qualifying conditions, that whoever caused his daughter to speak again should be her husband. A king's word is law; and if the king wants others to observe his laws, he must first keep them himself. Therefore the king must give me his daughter."

The councilor yelled, "Seize him and tie him up! Whoever says the king must do anything, insults his majesty, and is subject to being put to death. May it please your majesty to order this wrongdoer to be executed by the sword."

The king said, "Let him be executed."

After being tied up, Vanek was led to the place of his execution. Upon their arrival, Luck was waiting for him and said secretly to Intelligence: "See how this man has got on through you, until he has to lose his head! Make way, and let me take your place!"

As soon as Luck entered Vanek, the executioner's sword broke against the scaffold, just as if someone had snapped it; before they brought another, a trumpeter rode up from the city, galloping fast, and waving a white flag. Following the trumpeter was the royal carriage to fetch Vanek. The princess had told her father that Vanek was right, and the king's word should not be broken. Vanek might be of mean lineage, but the king could make him a prince.

The king agreed: "You're right; let him be a prince!"

Vanek was brought to the palace in the royal carriage and the councilors who had spoken against him were out of favor with the king. After the wedding, Vanek and the princess traveled down the road from the cathedral to the palace in their carriage. Intelligence was standing along the road and, seeing that he couldn't avoid meeting Luck, bent his head and cocked it to one side, just as though cold water had been thrown on him. It is said that from that time onward, Intelligence has always given a wide berth to Luck whenever he has had to meet him.

Moral: Even with thorough and intelligent planning, one can always use luck.

Based on: F. H. Lee, "Intelligence and Luck,"
Folk Tales of All Nations

Chapter 5

INDEFATIGABLE / UNSELFISH

In every part and corner of our life,
To lose oneself is to be the gainer;
To forget oneself is to be happy.

Robert Lewis Stevenson, "Old Mortality"

Ilyas's Search for Happiness

A farmer named Ilyas lived outside the town of Ufa in the former Soviet Republic of Bashkiria. When his father died, he was left in comfortable, but not wealthy, circumstances. His father had found him a bride the previous year, and Ilyas had inherited two cows, seven mares, and twenty sheep.

Ilyas was a good manager, and he and his wife, Sham-Shemagi, worked from dawn until dusk. He rose earlier than his neighbors and went to bed later than they did. He acquired more possessions and became richer every year. He worked hard for thirty-five years and accumulated a sizable fortune. He had fifty head of cattle, two hundred horses, and twelve hundred sheep. He had shepherds to tend the flocks and maidservants to milk the cows and make butter and cheese.

Ilyas's friends and neighbors envied his bountiful life. Visitors to his home came from far and near. He welcomed all of them and served his guests chowder, mutton, tea, and kumiss, made from fermented mares' milk. He killed a ram as soon as visitors arrived; if many came, he would kill two rams.

Ilyas had two sons and a daughter. He married off his sons and found a suitable husband for his daughter. When Ilyas was poor, his sons worked the fields and tended the herds. As he became wealthier, however, his sons grew lazy and spoiled. One of his sons began to drink excessively. His older son was killed in a fight, and his younger son married a proud woman and began to disobey his father. Ilyas asked him to leave.

Although Ilyas banished his son, he gave him a house and cattle, thus diminishing his own wealth. His sheep became ill with distemper, and many died. A year of famine followed. His hay was not worth harvesting, and many of his cattle died during the winter. Neighboring Kirgiz stole his best horses, reducing his property even further.

Ilyas's situation became increasingly dire. At age seventy, he was not the strong man that he had been. Finally, he had to sell his carpets, furs, saddles, and wagons. When he sold the last of his cattle, he was down to nothing. He and Sham-Shemagi had to hire out as servants. His younger son had moved to a distant land, and his daughter had died. No one was left to take care of them. All he had left were his clothes, shoes, slippers, hat, and fur greatcoat.

Their good neighbor, Muhamedshah, pitied them and offered to help, although he lived in modest circumstances himself. He had appreciated Ilyas's hospitality over the years and felt sorry for him. Muhamedshah said, "Come, Ilyas, and live with me—you and your old woman. In summer you can work for me in the garden, and in winter you can take care of the cattle; Sham-Shemagi may milk the mares and make kumiss. I will feed and clothe you both; whatever you need, tell me; I will give it."

Ilyas thanked his loyal neighbor, and he and his wife moved in as servants. Initially, it was difficult, but eventually they got used to it. They worked as hard as their strength permitted. Muhamedshah gained valuable service, because his servants had been masters themselves, and they knew how to keep everything in order. Muhamedshah was sorry to see people of high station reduced to such circumstances in life, however.

One day guests, kinsmen from a distant land, visited Muhamedshah. A Mullah, or Islamic priest / teacher, accompanied them. The host ordered a ram to be killed. Ilyas dressed the ram, cooked it, and served it to the guests. They ate the mutton and drank tea and kumiss. After dinner, the guests sat on down pillows and carpets and talked.

Ilyas had finished his chores and passed by the doorway. His neighbor saw him and asked his guests if they saw the old man walk by. One guest said that he had seen him and asked what was remarkable about him. Muhamedshah said, "This is remarkable—he was once our richest man. His name is Ilyas; maybe you have heard of him?" The guest admitted that he had heard of Ilyas, whose name was famous, but he had never seen him before. Muhamedshah told his guest that Ilyas had nothing left, was now a servant for him, and that he and his wife milked the cows.

Surprised, the guest observed that this showed how fortune sometimes moves in a circle; those at the top can end up at the bottom. The guest assumed that Ilyas felt bad about his change in fortune. Muhamedshah said it was difficult to tell; Ilyas lived quietly and did his work conscientiously. The guest asked to speak with the old man to ask him about his life. Muhamedshah asked Ilyas to bring in some kumiss and to ask his wife to come in with him.

Ilyas greeted the guests and his master, said a short prayer, and squatted by the doorway. His wife went behind the curtain with her mistress. Ilyas was given a cup of kumiss. He wished good health to the guests and his master, bowed, sipped the drink, and set it down. The guest asked Ilyas if he became depressed thinking about his past life, and if his present life was spent in sorrow reminiscing about what used to be.

Ilyas smiled and said that if he spoke about his previous fortune and subsequent misfortune, he would not believe him. Ilyas suggested that he ask his wife because, in the way of women, what is in her heart was on her tongue. She would tell the guest the entire truth of the matter.

Sham-Shemagi spoke from behind the curtain, "This is what I think about it: my old man and I have lived fifty years together. We sought happiness, but we did not find it. Now it is two years since we lost everything and have been living in service; we have found real happiness and ask for nothing better." The guests were surprised. Ilyas stood up and moved the curtain aside to look at his wife. She was standing with her arms folded. She smiled at her husband, and he smiled back.

Sham-Shemagi added, "I am speaking the truth, not jesting. We sought happiness for half a century, and as long as we were wealthy did not find it; but now that we have nothing left and are in service, we have found such happiness that we ask for nothing better." She was asked what constituted happiness for them now.

Sham-Shemagi said, "Well, in this: while we were rich, my old man and I never had an hour's rest. We never had time to talk, nor to think about our souls, nor to pray to God. There was nothing for us but care. When we had guests, it was a bother how to treat them, what to give them, so that they might not talk ill about us. Then, when the guests went away, we had to look after our work people; they would have to rest, they would have to be given enough to eat, and we would have to see that nothing that was ours would be lost—so we sinned.

"Then, again, there was worry lest the wolf would kill a colt or a calf, or lest thieves would drive off our horses. We would lie down to sleep but could not sleep for fear that the sheep would trample the lambs. We would go out, we would walk in the night; and at last, when we would get ourselves calmed down, then, again, there would be anxiety about getting food for the winter. Besides this, my old man and I never agreed. He would say we must do so, and I would say we must do so; and we would begin to quarrel—so we sinned. So we lived in worry and care and never knew happiness in life."

Sham-Shemagi concluded, "Now, when my old man and I get up in the morning, we always have a talk, in love and sympathy; we have nothing to quarrel about, nothing to worry about; our only care is to serve our master. We work according to our strength. We work willingly, so that our master may not lose, but gain. When we come in, we have dinner, we have supper, we have kumiss. If it is cold, we have heating fuel to burn and warm us, and we each have a sheepskin greatcoat. And we have time to talk and think about our souls and to pray to God. For fifty years, we sought happiness and only now have we found it!" The guests laughed.

Ilyas said, "Do not laugh, brothers; this thing is no jest, but human life. And the old woman and I were foolish when we wept over the loss of our property, but now God has revealed the truth to us; and it is not for our own consolation, but for your own good that we reveal it to you." The Mullah said, "This is a wise saying, and Ilyas has told the exact truth; and it is written in the Scriptures." The guests stopped laughing and were lost in thought.

Moral: Success and happiness cannot always be measured in economic terms.

Based on: Leo Tolstoy, "Ilyas," *Tolstoy: Tales of Courage and Conflict*

The Legend of the Two Discreet Statues

Centuries ago, a merry little fellow named Lope Sanchez lived in a small apartment in the Alhambra, the ancient palace and fortress of the Moorish monarchs in Granada. He worked in the gardens, was as active as a grasshopper singing all day long, and was the soul of the fortress. When his work was over, he would sit on one of the stone benches of the esplanade and strum his guitar and sing long ditties about El Cid and other heroes of Spain for the amusement of the old soldiers of the fortress. He would also strike up a merrier tune and set the girls dancing boleros and fandangos.

Like many small men, Lope Sanchez had a strapping, buxom

woman for a wife, who could almost have put him in her pocket. However, he lacked the usual poor man's lot—instead of ten children, he had only one. She was a little black-eyed girl, Sanchica, who was as merry as he and the delight of his heart. She played nearby as he worked in the gardens, danced to his guitar as he sat in the shade, and ran as wild as a fawn about the groves, alleys, and ruined walls of the Alhambra.

On the eve of the blessed St. John, holiday-loving men, women, and children of the Alhambra went up at night to the Mountain of the Sun to keep their midsummer vigil on its level summit. On a bright moonlit night, all the mountains were gray and silvery, and the city, with its domes and spires, lay in shadows below. On the highest part of the mountain, they lit a bonfire, according to an old custom handed down by the Moors. The inhabitants of the surrounding countryside kept a similar vigil, and bonfires along the folds of the mountains blazed in the moonlight.

An evening was passed dancing to the guitar of Lope Sanchez, who was never so joyous as when on a holiday revel of this kind. Little Sanchica and her friends played, gathering pebbles, among the ruins of an old Moorish fort that crowns the mountain. She found a small hand that was carved in dark black stone with the fingers closed and the thumb firmly clasped upon them. Overjoyed with her good fortune, she ran to her mother with her prize. It immediately became a subject of speculation and was viewed by some with superstitious distrust. One person said, "Throw it away; it is Moorish—depend upon it. There's mischief and witchcraft in it." Another said, "You may be able to sell it to the jewelers of Granada."

In the middle of this discussion was an old soldier, who had served in Africa and was as swarthy as a Moor. He said, "I have seen things of this kind among the Moors of Barbary. It is of great value to guard against the evil eye and all kinds of spells and enchantments. I give you joy, friend Lope; this will bring good luck to your child." Upon hearing this, Lope's wife tied the little carved hand to a ribbon and hung it around her daughter's neck.

The sight of this talisman called up all the favorite superstitions of the Moors. The dance was neglected, and the revelers sat in groups on the ground telling legendary tales handed down from their ancestors. Some of their stories turned upon the wonders of the very mountain upon which they were seated, which is a famous region of hobgoblins.

One old woman gave a long account of a subterranean palace in the bowels of the mountain, where Abu Abdallah, the last Moorish king of Granada, and all his Moslem court are said to remain enchanted. Pointing to some crumbling walls and mounds of earth on a distant part of the mountain, she said, "Among yonder ruins, a deep black pit goes down into the very heart of the mountain. For all the money in Granada, I would not look down into it.

"Once upon a time, a poor man of Alhambra, who tended goats upon this mountain, scrambled down into that pit after a young goat had fallen in. He came out again, all wild and staring, and told such things of what he had seen that everyone thought he had lost his mind. He raved for a day or two about hobgoblin Moors that had pursued him in the cavern, and he could only be persuaded with difficulty to drive his goats up the mountain again. He did so at last, but, poor man, he never came down again. Neighbors found his goats grazing around the Moorish ruins and his hat and coat lying near the mouth of the pit, but he was never heard of again."

Little Sanchica listened with breathless attention to this story. She was a curious child, and she immediately felt a great desire to peek into this dangerous pit. Quietly leaving her companions, she walked to the distant ruins, and, after strolling some time among them, came to a small basin near the brow of the mountain where it swept steeply into the valley of the Darro River. The mouth of the pit yawned in the center of this basin.

Sanchica ventured to the edge of the pit and peeked in. It was as black as pitch, and it looked bottomless. Her blood ran cold— she drew back—then peeked again—then considered running away—then took another peek—the very horror of it was a delight to her. She rolled a large stone over the brink. For some time, it fell in silence; then it struck some rocky projection with a violent crash. It then rebounded from side to side, rumbling and tumbling with a noise like thunder, then made a final splash into water, and all again was quiet.

This silence, however, did not continue for long. It sounded as though something had awakened within the dreary abyss. A murmuring gradually rose out of the pit like the hum and buzz of a beehive. It grew louder and louder. A confusion of voices as of a distant multitude could be heard, together with the faint din of arms, clash of cymbals, and blaring of trumpets, as if an army were marshaling for battle in the very bowels of the mountain.

Sanchica drew back in awe and hurried back to the place where she had left her parents and their companions. All were gone. The bonfire was going out, its last wreath of smoke curling up in the moonlight. The distant fires that had blazed along the mountains had all gone out. She called her parents and some of her companions by name but received no reply. Sanchica ran down the side of the mountain until she arrived in the alley of trees leading to the Alhambra, where she sat down on a shaded bench to recover her breath. The bell from the watchtower struck midnight.

Sanchica was being lulled to sleep by the quietness of the atmosphere, when her attention was caught by something glittering in the distance. To her surprise, she saw a long cavalcade of Moorish warriors pouring down the mountainside, moving through the leafy avenues. Some were armed with lances and shields, others with swords and battle-axes, all with polished breastplates that flashed in the moonlight. Their horses pranced proudly and champed at the bit, but they made no more sound than if they had been shod with felt shoes. The riders were as pale as death.

A beautiful lady with a crowned head and long golden locks entwined with pearls rode among them. Her horse was covered with crimson velvet embroidered with gold. She had a sad look on her face, and she kept her eyes fixed upon the ground. She was followed by a train of courtiers magnificently dressed in robes and turbans of diverse colors. In the middle of these, on a cream-colored charger, rode King Abu Abdallah in a royal robe covered with jewels and a crown sparkling with diamonds.

Little Sanchica knew him by his yellow beard and his resemblance to his portrait in a picture gallery she had visited. She looked on in wonder and admiration as this royal pageant passed. She knew that these monarchs, courtiers, and warriors were not real but things of magic or enchantment. Nevertheless, she looked on with a bold heart, deriving courage from the talisman that she wore around her neck.

After the cavalcade passed, Sanchica got up and followed. It continued to the great Gate of Justice, which stood wide open. The old invalid sentinels on duty lay on stone benches near the tower in profound and apparently charmed sleep. The phantom parade swept noiselessly by them with banners flying. To her surprise, Sanchica saw an opening in the earth within the tower, leading down beneath its foundation.

Sanchica entered and found steps crudely hewn in the rock and a vaulted passageway lit by silver lamps, which gave off a diffused light and a pleasant fragrance. Venturing farther, she came to a great hall carved out of the heart of the mountain, magnificently furnished in the Moorish style and lit by silver and crystal lamps. On an ottoman sat an old man in Moorish dress, with a long white beard, nodding and dozing, with a wooden staff in his hand. Near him sat a beautiful lady in ancient Spanish dress with a sparkling diamond coronet and hair entwined with pearls. She was playing softly on a silver lyre.

Sanchica recalled a story she had heard among the old people of the Alhambra about a Gothic princess confined in the center of the mountain by an old Arabian magician, whom she kept bound in sleep by the power of music. The lady paused with surprise at seeing a mortal in that enchanted hall. She asked, "Is it the eve of the blessed St. John?"

"It is," replied Sanchica.

The lady observed, "Then for one night, the magic charm is suspended. Come hither, child, and fear not. I am a Christian like you, though bound here by enchantment. Touch the fetters restraining me with the talisman that hangs around your neck, and for this night I shall be free."

The lady opened her robes and displayed a golden band around her waist and a golden chain that fastened her to the ground. The child applied the little black hand to the golden band and immediately the chain fell to the ground. At this sound, the old man awoke and began to rub his eyes; however, the lady ran her fingers over the strings of the lyre, and he began to nod and again fell into a slumber. The lady said, "Now touch his staff with the talismanic hand." Sanchica did so, and it slipped from his grasp; he fell into a deep sleep on the ottoman.

The lady gently laid the lyre on the ottoman next to the old man's ear. Then she strummed the strings. She said, "Oh potent spirit of harmony, continue to hold his senses enthralled until the return of the day." She continued, "Now follow me, my child, and you shall see the Alhambra as it was in the days of its glory, for you have a magic talisman that reveals all enchantments."

Sanchica followed the lady in silence. They passed through the entrance of the cavern in the tower of the Gate of Justice and on to the Plaza de las Algibes, the esplanade within the fortress. It was filled with Moorish soldiers, on foot and on horseback, marshaled in squadrons with banners displayed. Royal guards were also at the portal, along with rows of African blacks with drawn swords. No one spoke a word, and Sanchica fearlessly followed her guide.

Sanchica's astonishment increased on entering the royal palace, in which she had been reared. She hardly recognized it. Bright moonlight lit up all the halls, courts, and gardens almost as brightly as if it were daytime. The walls were no longer stained and aged by time. Instead of cobwebs, they were hung with rich silks of Damascus, and the gilded moldings and Arabesque paintings were restored to their original brilliancy. The halls, instead of being bare, were furnished with divans and ottomans decorated with the rarest materials. The fountains in the courts and gardens were all flowing.

The kitchens were in full operation; cooks were busy preparing shadowy dishes and roasting and boiling phantom pullets and partridges. Servants were busy passing silver dishes heaped with dainties and arranging a sumptuous banquet. The Court of Lions was thronged with guards and courtiers. At the upper end of the hall, in the salon of judgment, sat King Abu Abdallah on his throne, surrounded by his court and holding a shadowy scepter.

Despite the crowds and seeming bustle, not a voice or a footstep could be heard. Nothing interrupted the midnight silence but the splashing of the fountains. Little Sanchica followed her conductress in silent amazement about the palace, until they came to a portal opening to the vaulted passages beneath the great Tower of Comares. On each side of the portal sat the figure of a nymph, sculpted out of alabaster. The statues' heads were turned aside, with their gazes both fixed upon the same spot on the wall of the vault.

The enchanted lady paused, and called Sanchica over to her. She said, "Here is a great secret, which I will reveal to you for your faith and courage. These discreet statues watch over a mighty treasure hidden by a Moorish king. Tell your father to search the spot on which their eyes are fixed, and he will find what will make him richer than any man in Granada. Your hands alone, gifted as they are with the talisman, can remove the treasure. Tell your father to use it discreetly and to devote a part of it to the saying of daily Masses for my deliverance from this unholy enchantment."

The lady led Sanchica onward to the little garden of Lindaraxa, near the vault of the statues. The moon reflected on the waters of the solitary fountain in the center of the garden and shed a soft light on the orange and citron trees. The beautiful lady picked a branch of myrtle and wrapped it around the head of the child. She said, "Let this be a memento of what I have revealed to you and a testimonial of its truth. My hour has come; I must return to the enchanted hall. Do not follow me lest evil befall you. Remember what I have told you and have Masses said for my deliverance." The lady entered a dark passageway under the Tower of Comares and passed from view.

The faint crowing of a cock was now heard from the cottages below the Alhambra, in the valley of the Darro River, and a pale streak of light began to appear above the mountains to the east. A slight wind arose, and the rustling of dry leaves was heard through the courts and corridors. Door after door slammed shut. Sanchica returned to the halls, but King Abu Abdallah and his phantom court were gone.

The moon shone into empty halls and galleries stripped of their transient splendor, stained and dilapidated by time and hung with cobwebs. A bat flitted about in uncertain light, and a frog croaked from the fishpond. Sanchica made her way to a remote staircase that led up to the humble rooms occupied by her family. The door was open as usual, for Lope Sanchez was too poor to need a bolt or a bar. She crept quietly to her pallet, placed the myrtle wreath beneath her pillow, and fell asleep.

In the morning, Sanchica told her father about her experiences, but he didn't believe her. He told her it was all a dream, and he laughed at her for believing it. He went to work in the garden, but he had not been there long when his little daughter came running toward him, almost out of breath. She cried, "Father! Father! Behold the myrtle wreath that the lady wrapped around my head."

Lope Sanchez gazed in astonishment; the stalk of myrtle was of pure gold and every leaf was a sparkling emerald! Not being accustomed to precious stones, he didn't know the real value of the wreath, but he could tell it was more substantial than the stuff dreams are made of. He realized that the child had dreamed to some purpose. His first concern was to impose absolute secrecy upon his daughter. He need not have worried; she had discretion far beyond her years.

Then Lope Sanchez sneaked down unobserved to the vault containing the statues of the two alabaster nymphs. He noted that their heads were turned away from the portal, and that their eyes were fixed on the same point inside the vault. He admired this most discreet contrivance for guarding a secret. He followed the line from the eyes of the statues to the point on the wall where they were fixed, made a made a small mark on the wall, and left.

All day long, Lope Sanchez's mind was distracted. He could not help hovering in view of the statues and was nervous that the golden secret might be discovered. Every footstep that approached the place made him tremble. When he heard anyone approaching the place, he would leave, as though his lurking near the place would arouse suspicion. Then he would return and look on from a distance to see if everything was secure. Finally, to Lope Sanchez's relief, the long day drew a close. The sound of footsteps was no longer heard in the echoing halls of the Alhambra. The last stranger passed the threshold, and the great portal was barred and bolted.

Lope Sanchez waited until late at night before he ventured with his daughter to the hall of the two nymphs. He found them looking knowingly and mysteriously as ever at the secret place of deposit. As he passed between them, he thought: "Gentle ladies, I will relieve you from this charge that must have set heavily on your minds for the last two or three centuries." He chipped away at the part of the wall he had marked and opened a concealed recess, in which stood two porcelain jars.

Lope Sanchez tried to remove them, but they would not budge until touched by the innocent hands of his little daughter. With her help, he dislodged them from their niche and found to his great joy that they were filled with pieces of Moorish gold, mingled with jewels and precious stones. Before daylight, he carried them to his chambers and left the guardian statues with their eyes still fixed on the vacant wall.

Suddenly, Lope Sanchez had become a rich man, but riches, by their nature, brought a world of cares new to him. How was he to cash in his wealth safely? In fact, how was he to enjoy it without arousing suspicion? For the first time in his life, the fear of robbers entered his mind. He noted how insecure his apartment was and went to work barricading the door and windows. Even with these precautions, he could not sleep soundly.

Lope Sanchez's gaiety ended; he no longer had a joke or a song for his neighbors. He became the most miserable man in the Alhambra. His old friends noted the change in him, pitied him, and began to avoid him. They thought that he had become needy, and that they were in danger of his asking them for assistance. Little did they suspect that his problem was riches.

The wife of Lope Sanchez shared his anxiety, but she had religious comfort. Because Lope was a somewhat thoughtless little man, his wife was accustomed in all important matters to seek the counsel and ministry of her confessor, Friar Simon, a sturdy, broad-shouldered priest from the neighboring friary of San Francisco. He was, in fact, the spiritual comforter of half of the good wives in the neighborhood. Also, he was highly regarded by diverse sisterhoods of nuns, who repaid him for his religious comfort with dainties made in convents, such as confections, sweet biscuits, and bottles of spiced cordials, which he found to be marvelous restorers after fasts and vigils.

Friar Simon thrived in the exercise of his functions. The knotted rope around his waist indicated the austerity of his self-discipline. The multitudes doffed their caps to him as a mirror of his piety; even the dogs scented the odor of sanctity that came from his garments and howled from their kennels as he passed. Friar Simon, the spiritual counselor of the comely wife of Lope Sanchez, in his role as father confessor and domestic confidant of women in humble life in Spain, soon became acquainted, in great secrecy, with the story of the hidden treasure.

Friar Simon opened his eyes and mouth and crossed himself a dozen times at the news. After a moment's pause, he said, "Daughter of my soul, know that your husband has committed a double sin, a sin against the state and the church! The treasure he has seized for himself, being found in royal domains, belongs of course to the crown; however, being infidel wealth, rescued as it were from the very fangs of Satan, should be given to the church. Still, the matter may be accommodated. Bring the wreath to me."

When the good father saw the wreath, his eyes twinkled more than ever in admiration of the size and beauty of the emeralds. He said, "This, being the first fruits of this discovery, should be dedicated to pious purposes. I will hang it up as an offering before the image of San Francisco in our chapel and will earnestly pray to him this very night that your husband be permitted to remain in quiet possession of your wealth."

The good woman was delighted to make her peace with heaven at so cheap a price. The friar put the wreath under his robe and returned to his friary. When Lope Sanchez returned home, his wife told him about her conversation with Friar Simon. Lope was angry; he lacked his wife's devotion and had been concerned for some time with the visitations of the friar. He said, "Woman, what have you done? You have put everything at risk with your tattling."

She answered, "What! Would you forbid me to unburden my conscience to my confessor?"

Lope Sanchez replied, "No, wife! Confess as many of your own sins as you please; however, this digging up of the treasure is a sin of my own, and my conscience is very easy under the weight of it." Nothing would be gained by complaining. The secret was out, and, like water spilled in the sand, could not be undone. The only hope now was that the friar would be discreet. The next day, when Lope Sanchez was out, Friar Simon knocked on the door and entered with a subdued look on his face.

Friar Simon told Lope's wife, "Daughter, I have prayed earnestly to San Francisco, and he has heard my prayer. In the middle of the night, the saint appeared to me in a dream. He was frowning when he said, "Why do you pray to me to dispense with this treasure when you see the poverty of my chapel? Go to the home of Lope Sanchez and request in my name a portion of the Moorish gold to furnish two candlesticks for the main altar. Let him keep the rest of the treasure in peace."

When the good woman heard of this vision, she crossed herself with awe. She went to the hiding place of the treasure, filled a large leather purse with pieces of Moorish gold, and gave it to the friar. The pious friar bestowed benedictions upon her, took the purse, and left with an air of humble thankfulness. When Lope Sanchez heard of this second contribution to the church, he lost his temper. "Unfortunate man, what will become of me? I shall be robbed a bit at a time; I shall be ruined and have to resort to begging."

With difficulty, Lope Sanchez's wife tried to calm him down by reminding him of the considerable wealth that still remained, and how considerate it was of San Francisco to be satisfied with such a small portion. Unfortunately, Friar Simon had many poor relatives to be provided for, as well as a half dozen orphans and foundlings he had taken under his care. He repeated his visits every day with salutations in the name of Saint Dominick, Saint Andrew, and Saint James, until poor Lope was driven to despair.

Lope Sanchez knew that unless he got away from the holy friar, he would have to make offerings to every saint in the calendar. He decided to pack up his remaining wealth and leave in the middle of the night. He brought a stout mule and tethered it in a gloomy vault underneath the Tower of the Seven Floors—the place from which the Bellado, the goblin horse without a head, was said to come out at midnight to roam the streets of Granada, pursued by a pack of hell hounds.

Lope Sanchez did not believe the story, but he took advantage of the dread it caused; it was unlikely that anyone would visit the subterranean stable of the phantom steed during the night. During the day, he sent his family off to a distant village. After nightfall, he transferred his treasure to the vault under the tower, loaded his mule, and led it down the dusky avenue heading out of the city. Lope had made his plans with the utmost secrecy, telling only his wife and daughter.

Unfortunately, these plans became known to Friar Simon, who did not want these treasures to slip out of his grasp before he had one more chance at them for the benefit of the church and San Francisco. After evening bells, when all the Alhambra was quiet, Friar Simon crept out of the friary, went through the Gate of Justice, and concealed himself among the thickets of rose bushes and laurel that border the great avenue.

Eventually, Friar Simon heard the stomping of hoofs and saw an animal through the shadow of nearby trees. He tucked up the skirts of his habit, waited until his prey was directly in front of him, and vaulted onto the animal. He was barely astride when his mount began to kick and rear and plunge; he then set off at full speed down the hill. The friar attempted to check him but was unsuccessful. He bounced from rock to rock and from bush to bush; the friar's habit was torn to ribbons, and he received many hard knocks from branches of trees and scratches from brambles.

A pack of seven hounds in full cry at his heels added to his terror and distress. Worst of all, Friar Simon perceived too late that he was actually mounted on the terrible Bellado! They traveled at high speed down the great avenue across the Plaza Nueva and through city streets. Huntsman and hounds never made a more furious run or a more infernal uproar. In vain, the friar invoked every saint in the calendar and the Blessed Virgin as well. Every time he mentioned a holy name, the goblin steed jumped as high as a house as though he had been spurred. Throughout the night, Friar Simon was carried back and forth until every bone in his body ached.

Eventually, the crowing of a cock signaled the return of daylight. At that sound, the Bellado turned around and galloped back to his tower, retracing his route through city streets and across the Plaza Nueva. The seven dogs, yelling and barking, leaped up and snapped at the heels of the friar. The first streak of daylight had just appeared as they reached the tower. The goblin steed kicked up his heels, sent the friar somersaulting through the air, and plunged into the dark vault, followed by the infernal pack of dogs.

A peasant going to work the next morning found the unfortunate Friar Simon lying badly bruised under a fig tree at the foot of the tower, unable to speak or move. He was taken to his friary, where the story circulated that he had been set upon by robbers. He recovered the use of his limbs in two days. He consoled himself with the thought that although the mule with its treasures had escaped him, he had good pickings earlier.

Friar Simon's first act when he could move again was to search beneath his pallet, where he had hidden the myrtle wreath and the leather pouches of gold. To his dismay, he found that the wreath was now a withered branch of myrtle, and that the leather pouches were filled with sand and gravel. The chagrined friar had the discretion to hold his tongue. To tell his secret would cause him public ridicule and punishment by his superior. He did not reveal his midnight ride on the Bellado to his confessor until many years later on his deathbed.

For a long time, nothing was heard of Lope Sanchez. He was always remembered as a merry companion; however, it was feared that his melancholy conduct shortly before his mysterious departure had driven him to extreme measures.

Years later, one of his old companions, an invalid soldier, was knocked down and nearly run over by a coach and six horses. The carriage stopped, and a magnificently dressed old man stepped out to assist the poor invalid. The old soldier was astounded to learn that this grand cavalier was his old friend Lope Sanchez, who was celebrating the marriage of his daughter Sanchica to one of the first grandees of the land.

The wedding party waited inside Lope Sanchez's carriage. Dame Sanchez had grown as round as a barrel and was dressed in finery and jewels, with rings on every finger. Little Sanchica had grown into a beautiful, graceful young woman who could be mistaken for a duchess, if not a princess. The bridegroom, a withered, spindly-legged little man, was a Spanish grandee of true blue blood. The match had been of Sanchica's mother's making.

The heart of the honest Lope had not been spoiled by his riches. He kept his old comrade with him for several days, feasted him like a king, and took him to plays and bullfights. When the old soldier left, he took with him a bag of money for himself and another to be distributed among Lope's old comrades at the Alhambra.

Lope told everyone that a rich brother had died in America and left him heir to a copper mine; nevertheless, the shrewd gossips at the Alhambra insisted that his wealth was founded on his discovery of the secret guarded by the two alabaster nymphs of the Alhambra. These two discreet statues continue to the present day to have their eyes fixed on the same part of the wall, leading many to suppose hidden treasure remains. Others, particularly female visitors, regard them as lasting monuments to the fact that women can keep a secret.

Moral: Staying humble, even when elevated many levels above expectations, is a strong quality.

Based on: Washington Irving, "Legend of the Two Discreet Statues," *The Alhambra*

By Loving Man You Honor God

A rich man had three sons. Two left home to seek their fortunes in a distant city. One prospered, but the other was destitute. Years after they had left home, the father wrote a letter to the wealthy son inviting him and his brother to the wedding of their youngest brother.

The father wrote: "Return home, my son, and be sure to bring with you your poor brother so that we may all rejoice together. I promise to pay all traveling expenses that you incur in fulfilling the Commandment 'Honor thy father and mother.'"

The prosperous son immediately visited expensive shops where he outfitted himself, his wife, and his children. Then they began preparations for attending the wedding. When they were ready to depart, the wealthy son recalled that he had forgotten to invite his poor brother. He instructed his servants to call on his brother and bring him to his home quickly and to tell him that it was important.

The poor brother arrived out of breath and mentioned that he was surprised to be summoned after being ignored for years. His brother told him to ask no questions but just to get into the carriage. The poor brother did as he was told.

When they arrived at their parents' home, their father and all of the invited relatives came out of the house to welcome them. The rich son, dressed like a lord, was the first to step down from the carriage. He was followed by his wife and children, dressed in their expensive finery. Passers-by wondered who the prince was. The relatives told them that it was the son of the richest man in town, who was himself wealthy.

The poor brother, in his threadbare clothes and patched shoes, exited the carriage last. Again, passers-by asked who he was. The relatives were evasive in answering; they said that he was someone from the same city. When they asked if he were a brother or some other relative, they received no answer. As the new arrivals entered the house, they were greeted by musicians playing a joyful tune in their honor. The wedding guests happily sang, danced, and toasted the bride and bridegroom.

The rich son and his family stayed in his father's house for two weeks. Finally, the son said that his time was valuable and that he had to get back to his business. His father told him to do what was best for him. The son was surprised that although his father had promised to pay all his expenses, he did not say anything about it. So he prepared an itemized bill for his father, including his and his wife's and children's clothes, the cost of staying at inns, and miscellaneous expenses.

The father said, "How nice!" I am happy, my son, to see that you can afford such fine expensive clothes! May you, your wife, and children wear them in good health." The son reminded his father that he had promised to pay his expenses for the wedding.

The father was astonished and declared that he had made no such promise. Without commenting, the son handed his father the letter that he had sent and reminded his father that the promise was in his own handwriting. The father took the letter from his son and read it word for word: "I promise to pay all the traveling expenses that you may incur in fulfilling the Commandment, 'Honor thy father and mother.'" His son exclaimed, "There, you see!"

The father said, "Now just let us understand what it is I wrote to you. I promised to reimburse you for all the expenses that you would incur in fulfillment of the Commandment, 'Honor thy father and mother.' Had you really wished to honor me, you would have taken pity upon your poor brother and not brought him here dressed in tatters. You would have known the way to honor me was to clothe him decently. So you see that the expenses you incurred for the wedding were only for your own honor. And these, my son, I did not promise to pay for."

Moral: We do not honor God by outward display, but by caring
      for the less fortunate.

Based on: Nathan Ausubel, "By Loving Man You Honor God,"
      A Treasury of Jewish Folklore

The Maiden's Staircase

In the center of the Valencian plain in Spain lies the town of Mogente, split into two parts by the Bosquet River that flows through a valley between two massive mountains. Nearby on a promontory of large rocks that seem to have been piled up by some legendary hand, rises Montesa Castle, known for the military order from which it took its name. Orchards of carob trees and orange groves date from centuries ago when Moors controlled southern Spain.

On one of the mountains at the entrance to the town is a staircase of high and uneven steps, known as Escala de la Doncella, the Maiden's Staircase. The staircase has an ancient history dating back to Moorish times, when the wise and prudent Sidi Mohammed Ben Abderraman Ben Tahir was lord of Mogente and its fortress, which has long since fallen into ruins.

Ben Tahir was a cultivated man who appreciated literature and wrote poems. He enjoyed his rugged, provincial life and his books and poetry in the little spare time he had away from his duties as governor and warrior. The object of his greatest affection was a daughter who was being educated by a sage old man. Her name was Flor de los Jardines, Flower of the Gardens; he called her Flora. She was intelligent and pretty, and she loved nature. Ben Tahir built a tower for her connected to the castle by a long corridor that overlooked the beautiful countryside.

The old scholar taught Flora geography, history, and religion as well as the art of magic. As might be imagined, with her good looks and intelligence, Flora found great favor among knights her own age. Nevertheless, despite the admiration of her peers and her father fulfilling her every wish, she was melancholy and set in her ways. Her father did all he could to cheer her but to no avail. Finally, he decided to take her on a trip.

Ben Tahir and Flora visited the courts of Al-Andalus, where she attracted the attention of all the young knights. She had many suitors, but she rejected them all. She longed to return to her solitary tower, where she could lose herself in meditation. Ben Tahir noticed that Flora's tutor also was sad and spent long hours in deep thought.

When asked the reasons for Flora's and his sadness, the old scholar replied, "Allah keep you, oh noble Ben Tahir! You ask me the reasons for our sadnesses, and I must tell you that they arise from very diverse reasons. Your daughter is depressed because it is needful to fill her soul with love, as with any young lady; but she's so delicate and intelligent that she masters the arts and sciences exceptionally. She is so superior to the people who surround her that she can maintain no hopeful anticipation from any one of them. She knows more of the sciences than the scholars and, furthermore, knows herself to be more powerful than princes. Your daughter's ideal man does not exist in the world; nevertheless, she has not resigned herself to live without him.

In my case, the reason is very different. I feel my age more every day; I realize that my existence will stop any day now and quickly, and I would like to return to my home that my days might end in the country where I was born."

Ben Tahir was somewhat confused by the scholar's answer and did not wish to grant the him permission to leave without first consulting Flora. He explained to her what the old man had told him. Flora replied: "My father, in no way do I want the maestro to leave until he has told me the last and greatest of the several secrets he possesses, a secret, which, up until now, he has not wanted to reveal to me. As soon as he tells it to me, I shall be completely happy."

Ben Tahir told the old scholar about his conversation with Flora and her reply about wanting to know his last secret. The old man listened attentively and then said, "Flora's wish includes a very serious danger. Your daughter has discovered that the gigantic staircase cut into those nearby rocks leads to an enchanted palace, filled with wonders and dazzling opulence. The ascent by such high steps is impossible, for they were not made for mortal beings, for such poor creatures as ourselves. Consequently, It would be impossible to get into that celebrated palace if there were no other means to enter it."

Ben Tahir asked the scholar if another means of entering the palace existed. He acknowledged that it did exist, and that he knew it. The old man said that he had hesitated revealing it to Flora because of the preparation and the risk involved. Ben Tahir told him that he must reveal it to Flora or be put in jail for the rest of his life or even executed. The scholar warned Ben Tahir that the entrance he knew was so dangerous that Flora might remain in the enchanted palace for eternity.

Ben Tahir arranged that he and the old man would accompany Flora with some of his servants. He ordered that if he and his daughter did not return and the scholar was the only one to save himself, the servants would cut his head off. The old tutor agreed to meet them at the foot of the staircase at dawn to go with them.

Ben Tahir and Flora arrived at the foot of the staircase early, at midnight; the old magician was already there, reading an ancient book by candlelight. The maestro read in a high-pitched voice. When he had completed reading the first page, a terrifying rumble was heard from the underground. As the old man continued to read, the rumble grew louder. After he completed the second page, a huge crevice opened in the side of the mountain.

Ben Tahir and Flora were overcome by fear. The old man kept reading, and, when he had finished the third page, the enormous cleft grew wider. The walls of rock were split as though by a magic power. Inside, a magnificent palace could be seen; glittering lights illuminated the most fabulous treasures that could be imagined. Gilded roofs were supported by emerald columns, and the walls were studded with precious stones.

The old man took out a pipe and blew on it. Ben Tahir and his daughter hurried inside the marvelous palace with him. The scholar continued to read words, incomprehensible to them, from the ancient book. After an hour had passed, the maestro whistled again on the pipe. He, Ben Tahir, and Flora ran to the exit. When they were outside the mountain, the rocks closed behind them with the sound of an erupting volcano.

The lord of Mogente and his daughter were overwhelmingly happy, although they kept secret from everyone the marvels they had seen. The old scholar was granted permission to return home for his remaining years on the condition that he give the magic book to Flora. Ben Tahir and Flora kept it safe.

Years passed, and Flora and her father considered themselves fortunate to possess the key to entering the impressive fortress. One day, Ben Tahir found that his daughter was missing. He ordered the palace to be searched, but no one could find her. When interrogated, her servants revealed that she had been seen leaving the palace with only one servant, whom she had ordered to remain at the foot of the rocky stair. Hours passed, and Flora did not return.

Ben Tahir needed no further explanation. He raced to the stairs and desperately called out to his daughter. From within the earth, he heard a pitiful moan, then another; it was Flora's voice. Ben Tahir ordered all of his servants and slaves to demolish the staircase and to raze the mountain. As the exhausted workers dug deeper, Flora's voice grew weaker and weaker. The moans motivated them to dig until all of the workers dropped with exhaustion.

Ben Tahir decided that only magic could help him now. He

sailed for Africa to visit the old magician, who lived in Mequinez. When he arrived at the old man's house, he found him in bed at the point of death. The maestro tried to be gracious to his old master but was unable to be of much help. He could barely reply, haltingly, that his magic science was not sufficient to disenchant Flor de los Jardines. After saying this, he died. Ben Tahir, worn out with grief, died of sorrow the following day.

Old men of Mogente say that Flora's wailing and lamentation are still heard, particularly around midnight. For centuries, there have been rumors of an incredible apparition, which the oldest men in the town affirm on their strongest oaths, of a very beautiful woman dressed in exquisite finery and wearing brilliant jewels. She descends the staircase as though she were royalty and waits for a simple mortal to approach her with the intent of disenchanting her. For six centuries, no one has been able to do that, despite the fact that any man who would succeed could be married to an extremely lovely young woman.

Perhaps it is only a vain longing, or perhaps it is true. Unfortunately, the daughter of Ben Tahir must remain enchanted for all eternity.

Moral: Be careful what you wish for; you may get it. Sometimes
    we should be satisfied with what we have.

Based on: Antonio Jimenez-Landi, "The Maiden's Staircase,"
    The Treasure of the Muleteer and Other Spanish Tales

How Much Land Does a Man Need?
An elder sister came from her town in Russia to visit her younger sister in the country. The elder sister was married to a merchant and the younger to a peasant in the village. The two sisters sat down and talked over a cup of tea. The elder sister boasted about the superiority of town life, with all its comforts, fine clothes, and fancy food and drink, as well as the parties and visits to the theater. Resenting this attitude, the younger sister scoffed at the life of a merchant's wife.

The younger sister added, "I wouldn't like to change my life for yours. I admit that mine is dull, but at least we have few worries.

You live in grander style, but you must have a sufficient amount of business or you'll be ruined. One day you are rich, and the next day you might find yourself out in the street. Here in the country, we don't have those ups and downs. A peasant's life may be poor, but it's long. Although we may never be rich, we'll always have enough to eat."

The elder sister then stated her mind: "Enough to eat, indeed, with nothing but those filthy pigs and calves! What do you know about nice clothes and good manners? No matter how hard your husband slaves away, you'll spend your lives in the muck, and that's where you'll die. The same goes for your children."

The younger sister retorted, "What of it? That's how it is here. At least we know where we stand. We don't have to crawl and beg to anyone, and we're afraid of no one. You are surrounded by temptations in town. All may be well one day, but the next day the Devil tempts your husband with cards, women, and drink. Then you're ruined. It happens, doesn't it?"

Pakhom, the younger sister's husband, was resting in the back of the room listening to the women's conversation. He admitted, "It's true what you say. Ever since I was a youngster, I've been too busy tilling the soil to let that kind of nonsense enter my mind. My only gripe is that I don't have enough land. Give me enough land, and I'll fear no one—not even the Devil himself." The sisters finished their tea, talked a little longer about dresses, put the dishes away, and went to bed.

Unfortunately, the Devil had been sitting behind the stove and had heard everything. He was delighted that a peasant's wife had caused her husband to boast that if he had enough land, he would fear no one. He thought, "Good. I'll have a little game with you. I'll see that you have plenty of land; that way I'll get you in my clutches!"

A lady with a small estate of three hundred acres lived just outside the village. She maintained good relations with the peasants and never mistreated them. To manage her estate, she hired an old soldier who harassed the peasants by frequently imposing fines. No matter how careful Pakhom was, one of his horses might stray into his neighbor's oats, or a cow might wander into her garden, or some calves would venture into her meadows. On every occasion, he would have to pay a fine.

Pakhom would pay the fine and then swear at his family when he arrived home. He was bothered by this all summer. He welcomed winter because his animals were kept in a shed. He begrudged paying for fodder, but at least he no longer had to pay fines when they had strayed. That winter, Pakhom heard that his neighbor lady wanted to sell some of her land.

A few peasants, speaking for village community, begged the lady to sell her land to them. The peasants considered buying the entire estate. They met once and then again but made no progress. The Devil had set them against one another, and nothing could be agreed upon. Finally, they decided to buy the land in separate lots, each according to what he could afford. The lady agreed to this.

Pakhom learned that one of his neighbors was buying fifty acres, and that the lady had taken half payment, allowing the buyer to pay the balance in one year. Pakhom was envious. He was worried that his neighbors would buy up all of the land, leaving nothing for him. He talked to his wife about it. He said, "Everyone's buying land. We must get hold of at least twenty acres or we won't be able to live, with the manager assessing fines."

Pakhom and his wife thought long and hard about how to buy the land. They had only a hundred rubles saved, so they would have to sell a foal and half their bees, hire out one of their sons to work for someone who paid wages in advance, and borrow from a brother-in-law to accumulate half the price. Pakhom took the money, chose thirty acres of partly wooded land, and went to see the lady and make a deal. He bought the land by paying half down and agreeing to pay the balance within two years.

Pakhom borrowed money for seeds and sowed his recently purchased land; the harvest was bountiful. Within a year, he had repaid the lady and his brother-in-law. He was now a landowner in the full sense of the word: he plowed and sowed his own fields, reaped his own hay, cut his own timber, and pastured cattle on his own land.

Pakhom lived a landowner's life and was happy. Unfortunately, the neighboring peasants trespassed on his cornfields and meadows. At first, he spoke to them politely about this, but they continued to let their cows stray onto his meadows and their horses wander through his corn. He drove them out without taking further action, but finally he lost patience and complained to the District Court. He knew the peasants were not doing it deliberately, but because they were short of land. Nevertheless, he thought, "I can't let this go on. Before long, they'll have destroyed all I have. I must teach them a lesson."

Pakhom taught them a lesson in court, and then another, making them pay fines. His neighbors resented this. They continued to let their cattle stray on his land, now on purpose. One night, someone cut down ten trees in Pakhom's woods for their bark. The next day, when he was riding through his woods, he saw tree trunks lying all around, stripped of their bark, with the stumps lying nearby. Pakhom was angry to see that only one tree in that section of his woods had been left standing.

Pakhom thought for awhile and decided that it must be his neighbor Semyon who was doing this. He went over and searched Semyon's place but found nothing. The visit resulted in the two men swearing at each other. Pakhom was convinced of Semyon's guilt, so he filed a formal complaint. The magistrates acquitted Semyon for lack of evidence. This angered Pakhom even more, causing a stormy meeting with the village elder and the magistrates. Pakhom fell out with the magistrates as well as his neighbors, who threatened to burn his cottage down. Although Pakhom now had plenty of room, he felt that the community was closing in on him.

Rumors began to circulate that many peasants were leaving to settle in other parts of the country. One day a peasant who was traveling through the region stopped at Pakhom's for the night. The traveler told Pakhom that he had come from the South, from the other side of the Volga River. He told his host that many people from his own village had settled there. They joined the commune and had been allocated twenty-five acres of land each. He told Pakhom, "The land is so fertile that rye grows as high as a horse, and it's so thick you can make a whole sheaf from five handfuls! One peasant arrived there with one kopeck and his bare hands to work with, and now he has six horses and two cows."

This news excited Pakhom. He thought: "Why should I struggle to earn a living hemmed in here, when I could be leading a good life somewhere else? I could sell the land and cottage here and with the money build a house there and start a new farm. I must go and find out what it's like for myself."

When summer came, Pakhom traveled down the Volga by steamboat, then walked the remaining three hundred miles to the new settlement. It was just as the visitor had described it. By autumn, when Pakhom had found out all he needed to know, he returned home. He sold his land, home, and cattle at a profit, resigned from the commune, and waited until spring; then he left with his family for the new settlement.

When Pakhom arrived in the South with his family, he managed to get on the register of a large village commune. He was granted a hundred acres in addition to the use of the communal pasture. He erected buildings and stocked his farm with cattle. The allotted land was three times what he had at home and was ideal for growing corn. He had plenty of arable land and pasturage and was able to keep as many cattle as he wanted.

At first, everything seemed fine; nevertheless, when he had settled into his new life, he felt cramped again. During the first year, he had sown wheat, and the crop had been excellent. When he wanted to sow more wheat, he realized he needed more land. Unfortunately, some of his allotted land was not suitable for wheat. In the South, wheat is sown only on grassland or on fallow land. It is sown for two or three years on a plot of land and then the land is left fallow until overgrown with feather grass again.

There wasn't enough this type of land to fill the demand, so people fought over it. The richer ones sowed their own, and the poorer ones mortgaged theirs to merchants to pay their taxes. Pakhom wanted to sow more wheat, so, the following year, he leased fields from a dealer for one year. He sowed a lot of wheat and had a bumper crop. Unfortunately, the fields were a long way from the village, and the wheat had to be carted more than ten miles. Pakhom noticed that some peasant farmers with large homesteads in the neighborhood were becoming wealthy. He thought, "What if I bought some freehold land and built a homestead like theirs? Then the crops would not have to be carted so far."

Pakhom farmed this way for three years, leasing land and sowing wheat. He saved some money in these good crop-growing years. However, he grew tired of leasing land, year after year, and hauling crops great distances. In his third year, Pakhom and a merchant each paid half on a plot of pasture land that they purchased from peasants.

Pakhom was later told of a peasant who had purchased thirteen hundred acres, had gone bankrupt, and was selling the land cheaply. Pakhom bargained with him and finally agreed upon fifteen hundred rubles, half down, half to be paid later. The deal was all but closed, when a passing merchant stopped at Pakhom's farm to have his horses fed. They talked over tea. The merchant told Pakhom that he was returning from the distant land of the Bashkirs, where he had bought thirteen thousand acres for one thousand rubles.

The merchant told Pakhom: "All I had to do was give the old men there a few presents — a few hundred rubles worth of silk robes and carpets, a chest of tea, and vodka for anyone who wanted it. I managed to get the land for twenty kopecks an acre. The land is near a river, and it is all beautiful grassy steppe. There's so much land you couldn't walk around it in a year. It all belongs to the Bashkirs. The people there aren't very smart; you can get land from them for practically nothing." Pakhom thought, "Why should I pay fifteen hundred rubles for thirteen hundred acres and load myself down with debt? Think what I could buy with the same money down there."

Pakhom asked for directions to the land of the Bashkirs and prepared to leave. He took one workman with him and stopped in town to buy a chest of tea, vodka, and other presents as the merchant had advised. He reached the Bashkir settlement in seven days. It was as the merchant had described. The people lived on the steppe, near a river, in tents of thick felt. They didn't farm the soil, and their cattle, horses, and sheep wandered around the steppe. The men only seemed interested in drinking tea and kumiss, eating, and playing their pipes. The Bashkirs seemed ignorant and knew no Russian, but they were friendly people.

When the Bashkirs saw Pakhom coming, they rushed out of their tents to greet him. An interpreter was found, and Pakhom told them that he had come to buy land. They welcomed him, took him to one of their largest tents, and invited him to sit with them on thick cushions while they offered him tea and kumiss. They slaughtered a sheep and fed him mutton. Pakhom brought the presents in from his cart and shared the tea and vodka. The Bashkirs talked among themselves and then asked the interpreter to translate.

The interpreter said, "They want me to tell you that they have taken a liking to you, and that it is their custom to do all they can to please a guest and repay him for his gifts. You have given them presents, so please tell them what they can do to show their gratitude." Pakhom replied, "What I like most of all here is your land. Back home, there isn't enough land to satisfy everyone, and, furthermore, the soil is exhausted. You have plenty of land here, and it looks very fertile. I've never seen soil like it."

The interpreter translated, and the Bashkirs talked among themselves. Although Pakhom did not know what they were saying, they were cheerful and laughing. The interpreter said, "I'm to tell you that they would be pleased to let you have as much land as you like for your kindness. All you have to do is point it out, and it shall be yours; however, some of them are saying that they should first consult the elder about the land."

While the Bashkirs were talking, a man in a fox-fur cap entered the tent, and everyone became quiet and stood up. The interpreter explained to Pakhom that he was the elder. Pakhom immediately presented his best robe and five pounds of tea to the elder, who accepted the gifts and sat in the place of honor. The Bashkirs explained something to the elder, who motioned them to be quiet and spoke to Pakhom in Russian. He told Pakhom that their offer was all right, and that he could choose whatever land he liked because there was plenty of it.

Pakhom wondered how these arrangements could be made formal. After all, he wouldn't want them to change their minds in the future. He replied, "Thank you for your kind words. Yes, you do have a great deal of land, but I only need a little; however, I would like to be sure which will be mine, so couldn't it be measured and transferred to me by some sort of contract? Our lives are in God's hands, and although you good people are willing to give me land now, it's possible your children might want it back again."

The elder agreed to have a contract drawn up. Pakhom said, "I've heard that you transferred some land to a merchant not long ago, together with the title deeds. I would like you to do the same with me." The elder said that it would not be a problem. They could ride into town to see the clerk and have the documents properly witnessed and signed. Pakhom asked about the price of land, and was told that there was a fixed price — a thousand rubles a day. He asked what kind of a price that was, and how many acres that would be.

The elder told Pakhom, "We don't do things your way. We sell land by the day. However much land you can walk around in one day will be yours. And the price is one thousand rubles a day."

Pakhom was amazed and observed, "A man can walk around a lot of land in one day." The elder laughed and agreed: "All of it will be yours, but there is one condition: if you don't return to your starting point the same day, your money will be forfeited."

Pakhom asked how he could mark where he had been. The elder told him, "We'll all go to the place that you select and wait until you have completed your circuit. You must take a spade, dig a hole at every turn, and leave the turf piled up. Afterwards, we will go from hole to hole with a plow. You may make as large a circuit as you like, only you must be back at your starting point by sunset. All the land you can walk around will be yours."

Pakhom was delighted, and an early start was agreed upon. At nightfall, they made up a feather-bed for Pakhom and left. They promised to ride out to the selected starting point before sunrise.

Pakhom lay down on the feather-bed but could not sleep; the thought of all that land kept him awake. He thought: "Tomorrow, I shall mark out a really large stretch. In one day, I can easily walk thirty-five miles. The days are long now—just think how much land I'll have from walking that distance. I'll sell the poorer pieces or lease it to the peasants. I'll take the best for myself and farm it. I'll have two ox-plows and hire two laborers to use them. I'll cultivate a hundred and fifty acres and let the cattle graze the rest."

Pakhom could not sleep until just before dawn. The moment he fell asleep, he had a dream. He seemed to be lying in the same tent and could hear some laughter outside. Pakhom went outside to see who was laughing and found the Bashkir elder there, holding his sides and rolling about in fits of laughter. Pakhom asked him what he was laughing at, and saw that it wasn't the elder but the merchant who had called on him and told him about the land. When Pakhom asked him if he had been there long, the merchant turned into the peasant who had come up from the Volga and visited him.

Then Pakhom saw that it wasn't the peasant, but the Devil himself, with horns and hoofs, sitting there laughing his head off. In front of him lay a barefoot man wearing only a shirt and trousers. Pakhom took a closer look and saw that the man was dead, and that it was he. He woke up in a cold sweat and wondered about the source of dreams.

Pakhom looked around and saw that it was getting light at the open door; dawn was breaking. He aroused his workman and ordered him to harness the horse. The two went off to wake the Bashkirs.

The Bashkirs started out, some on horses, others in carts. Pakhom traveled in his cart with his workman, taking a spade with him. They came out onto the open steppe just as the sun was rising and climbed a small hill. The Bashkirs gathered in one place. The elder went over to Pakhom, pointed, and said, "Look, that's all ours, as far as the eye can see. Choose any part you like." Pakhom was eager, for the land was all virgin soil, as flat as the palm of one's hand, as black as poppy seed, with different kinds of grass growing in the hollows.

The elder took off his fox-fur cap and placed it on the ground. He told Pakhom, "Let this be the marker; this is the starting point to which you must return. All the land you can walk around will be yours." Pakhom took out his money and placed it on the cap. He took off his outer coat, tightened his belt, and stuffed a small bag of bread in his shirt. He tied a water flask to his belt, pulled up his boots and took the spade from his workman.

Pakhom could not decide in which direction to go; the land was good in every direction. He decided to walk toward the sunrise. He faced east and waited for the sun to appear above the horizon. As soon as he saw the sun's rays, he put the spade on his shoulder and walked out onto the steppe. He walked steadily; after he had gone three quarters of a mile, he stopped, dug a hole, and piled the pieces of turf on top of one another so that they were visible. The stiffness was gone from his legs, so he lengthened his stride. He stopped a little further on and dug another hole.

When Pakhom looked back, he could see the small hill in the sunlight with the people standing on it. He estimated that he had covered three miles. He was warm, so he took off his undercoat, flung it over his shoulder, and walked another three miles. He thought: "Well, that's the first stretch completed! But there are four to a day, and it's too early to begin turning. I must take these boots off, though."

Pakhom took off his boots, hung them from his belt, and moved on. The going was easier now, and he thought, "I'll do another three miles and then turn left. The land is so beautiful here, it would be unfortunate to lose any of it. The further I go, the better the land gets." He continued to walk straight ahead. When he looked back at the hill; the people on it were barely visible.

Pakhom decided that he had walked far enough in one direction. He was hot and thirsty, so he stopped, dug a hole, piled up the turf, drank from his flask, and took a sharp left turn. The grass was higher, and it was very hot walking through it. He was getting tired. He looked up at the sun and saw that it was noon. He needed a rest, so he sat down and had some bread and water. He did not stretch out. He knew if he did, he would fall asleep. The food had given him strength, but the extreme heat was making him sleepy.

Pakhom had walked a long way in the same direction and was just about to turn left again when he noticed a lush hollow and decided that it would be a pity not to claim it. It would be a great place to grow flax. He walked around the low-lying meadows, dug a hole on the other side, and then turned the second corner. He looked back and could barely see the people on the hill. They were at least ten miles away. He decided that the first two sides were too long, and that he should make the third side shorter.

Pakhom quickened his step on the third side. He noticed that the sun was already half way to the horizon, and he had completed only one mile on the third side. The starting point was still ten miles away, but he decided to head back there, even though his plot of land would be lopsided. It realized that he shouldn't try to grab too much land. He hastily dug another hole and turned back toward the hill.

Pakhom found the going difficult on the way back. He was exhausted from the heat, his bare feet were cut and bleeding, and his legs were giving out. He wanted to rest, but he knew that he couldn't stop and still get back by sunset. The sun was sinking lower and lower. He wondered: "Have I blundered, trying to take too much? What if I'm not back in time?" The hill was far off; the sun was close to the horizon.

Pakhom struggled. He walked faster and faster, but there was still a long way to go. He started to run and threw away his coat, boots, flask, and cap, keeping only the spade. He was afraid that he had been too greedy, that he would never make it back by sunset. His fear made him even more breathless. He ran on, his shirt and trousers clinging to him with perspiration. His throat was parched, his lungs were puffing like bellows, his heart beating like a hammer, and his legs did not seem to be his. He was terrified and thought: "All this strain will be the death of me."

Although he feared death, he could not stop. He thought that he would be called an idiot for stopping after coming all this way. He ran on until he could hear the Bashkirs shouting and cheering him on. Their shouts spurred him on even more, so he summoned his last ounce of strength and kept running. The sun was almost touching the horizon; it was large, blood red, and shrouded in mist. It was about to set, but he was not far from the starting point either.

Pakhom could see the people on the hill now, waving their arms and encouraging him. He could see the fur cap on the ground and the money on it. He could also see the elder sitting there with his arms pressed to his sides. Then Pakhom remembered his dream. He thought: "I've plenty of land now, but will God let met live to enjoy it? No, I'm finished. I'll never make it."

Pakhom looked at the sun. It had reached the earth now. Half of the great circle was below the horizon. With all the strength he had left, he lurched forward, hardly able to keep himself from falling. He reached bottom of the hill, and suddenly everything had become dark. The sun had set. Pakhom groaned and thought that all his effort had been in vain. He wanted to stop, but he heard the Bashkirs cheering him on.

Pakhom realized that at the bottom of the hill, the sun had set, but it had not for those at the top. He took a deep breath and rushed up the hill. When he reached the top, he saw the cap with the elder sitting by it, holding his sides and laughing his head off. Then he remembered the dream and groaned. His legs gave way, he fell forward and just managed to reach the cap with his hands. The elder exclaimed, "Well done! You have earned yourself a lot of land!"

Pakhom's workman ran up and tried to lift his master, but blood flowed from his mouth. He was dead. The Bashkirs clicked their tongues in sympathy. Pakhom's workman picked up the spade, dug a grave for his master, and buried him.

Moral: Greed is not a desirable trait. Blatant greed can be the death of you.

Based on: Leo Tolstoy, "How Much Land Does a Man Need?"
   How Much Land Does a Man Need? and Other Stories

Chapter 6

RESOLUTE / COURAGEOUS

Courage is the conqueror of men;
Victorious both over them and in them;
The iron will of one stout heart
Shall make a thousand quail;
A feeble dwarf, dauntlessly resolved,
Will turn the tide of battle,
And rally to a nobler strife
The giants that had fled.

Martin Tupper, *Proverbial Philosophy of Faith*

The Christ of the Skull

Centuries ago in Spain, the King of Castile was going to war with the Moors, enemies of the Christian faith. He sent a martial summons to all of his noblemen to aid the cause. The streets of Toledo resounded night and day with the military sounds of drums and trumpets. In the gateways to Visagra and Cambron as well as in the narrow entrance to the bridge of St. Martin's, not an hour passed without the cry of sentinels announcing the arrival of a knight who, preceded by his banner and followed by his horsemen and foot soldiers, had come to join the main body of the Castilian army.

Before taking the road to the frontier, the gathered knights attended public entertainments, lavish feasts, and colorful tournaments. A grand ball at the palace closed the festivities on the evening before the day appointed by His Highness for the army to set out. A motley crowd of pages, soldiers, crossbowmen, and hangers-on gathered around huge bonfires in the spacious courtyards. Some were grooming their horses and polishing their arms for combat. Others were wailing and blaspheming their ill luck with the dice.

Some were led by a minstrel accompanied by a crude violin in singing a martial ballad. Still others were buying good-luck pieces blessed by the touch of the sepulcher of Santiago, laughing at the antics of a clown, practicing on trumpets, or telling stories of chivalry, love, or recently performed miracles.

Above the sound of martial music, one could hear blacksmiths pounding anvils, the stamping of horses' hoofs, loud voices, uncontrolled laughter, intemperate oaths, and other discordant sounds. Also, floating in the air was the distant music of the ball in the second story salons of the palace. The activities in the salons, if not as varied as those in the courtyards, were more dazzling and magnificent. In the great halls, silk and gold tapestries depicted scenes of love, the chase, and war. Galleries were adorned with trophies of arms and shields with coats of arms lighted by lamps and candelabras of bronze, silver, and gold.

Everywhere one looked, beautiful ladies in rich garments glided around the dance floor. Nets of pearl enclosed their tresses, ruby necklaces blazed upon their breasts, veils of white lace caressed their cheeks, and fans with ivory handles hung from their wrists. Their dancing partners were gallants with velvet sword belts, brocaded jackets, silken trousers, daggers with ornamental hilts, and highly polished swords.

That bright and shining assemblage of youthful cavaliers and ladies was viewed by their elders seated in chairs surrounding the royal dais. One young woman had attracted attention for her incomparable loveliness. She had been hailed as Queen of Beauty in all the tournaments and courts, and her colors had been adopted by the most valiant knights as their emblem; her charms were the theme of troubadours' songs, and she was the one toward whom all eyes turned with admiration.

The most illustrious sons of the nobility of Toledo gathered around her with eagerness, as though they were humble vassals in the train of their mistress. These gallants were always in the retinue of this celebrated beauty, Dona Ines de Tordesillas, and were never discouraged in their suit by her haughty and disdainful manner. One was charmed by a smile, another by a gracious look, a third by a flattering word. Each looked for the slightest sign of preference, thought that he detected a vague promise, and hoped that he would be her choice.

Two of these young gallants were considered the favorites for her attention and the farthest advanced upon the pathway to her heart. These two knights, Alonso de Carrillo and Lope de Sandoval, were equals in birth, valor, and chivalric accomplishments. Both were natives of Toledo; they had first borne arms together. They were attracted to Dona Ines on the same day, and both developed a hidden and ardent love for her. Their love grew in secrecy and silence until, inevitably, their actions and conversation betrayed their unannounced love.

During the day at the tournaments in the Zocodover, the central square of the city, as well as at the games of the court or any other opportunity to display gallantry or wit, these knights were eager to win distinction in the eyes of their lady. At night, they exchanged their helmets for plumes and their chain mail for brocade and silk and stood together near her in the salons, where they engaged in a contest of exquisite phrases and ingenious replies.

Lesser gallants gathered around and cheered on the strife created by their two comrades. The fair lady would approve with a faintly perceptible smile their flashes of wit flattering her vanity. She enjoyed it most when each gave a sharp reply aimed at the perceived vulnerable point of his rival, his self-love. The courtly combat of wit and gallantry was gradually growing fiercer, still civil but accompanied by a curving of lips in a smirk and the flashing of eyes that failed to conceal the repressed anger that raged in the breasts of the rivals.

Recognizing that the tension must be broken, Dona Ines rose to make a tour of the salons. Whether intentionally or not, the lady had let one of her perfumed gloves fall from her lap. All of the knights around her made an attempt to pick it up, and a vain smile appeared on the lips of the haughty Dona Ines. With a lofty manner, she reached out her hand for the glove toward Lope and Alonso, who were closest to it. Both young men stooped and picked up the glove, each holding one end.

Lope and Alonso, looking defiantly at each other, were immovable and determined not to give up the glove they had just picked up. The lady let out a light, involuntary cry; the astonished spectators began to murmur. The threatening scene in the presence of the king might be considered a serious breach of courtesy. The young men remained motionless and mute, looking at each other but indicating no sign of the tempest in their souls except for a slight tremor that rippled through their limbs.

The murmurs and exclamations were reaching a climax. People moved to group themselves around the principal actors in the drama. Dona Ines, either in bewilderment or in delight, was moving back and forth as if seeking refuge from the eyes of the crowd. Catastrophe now seemed inevitable. The two young men exchanged words in an undertone and, still holding the glove in a tight grip, seemed to be seeking the hilts of their daggers.

Suddenly, the crowd opened up, and the king appeared. He was tranquil; his bearing indicated neither indignation nor anger. He surveyed the scene; one glance was enough to put him in command of the situation. He withdrew the glove from the young men's hands, who released it without hesitation. Turning to Dona Ines de Tordesillas, who was leaning on the arm of a duenna and appeared about to faint, the king, with a firm though controlled voice, handed her the glove, saying, "Take it, senora, and be careful not to let it fall again, lest when you recover it, you find it stained with blood." By the time the king had finished speaking, Dona Ines had fainted into the arms of the women attending her.

Alonso and Lope, the former crushing his velvet cap in his hands and the latter biting his lips until the blood came, fixed each other with a stubborn, intense stare. In this crisis, a stare was the equivalent to a blow, a glove thrown in the face, or a challenge to mortal combat.

The king and queen retired to their chambers at midnight. The ball was over, and townspeople who wanted to see the nobility in their finery gathered around outside the palace and in the Zocodover. For an hour or two, activity reigned, including squires on steeds with fancy saddles and harnesses, masters-at-arms in showy vestments, drummers dressed in bright colors, soldiers in glistening armor, pages in velvet cloaks and plumed hats, and foot-men preceding richly decorated chairs and litters. Footmen carried blazing torches casting a rosy glow upon the crowds, who watched the nobility of Castile passing by.

Finally, the commotion subsided, and the crowd dispersed into the darkening labyrinth of streets and alleys. The silence of the night was broken by the distant cry of a sentinel and the clang of bolts and bars on gates being closed.

At the top of the stone stairway leading to the palace, a knight appeared, who, after looking around for someone, slowly descend-ed to the Cuesta del Alcazar and made his way to the Zocodover. In the city square, he stopped for a moment and looked around again. The night was dark—not one star shone in the sky, and the square was poorly lit. Eventually, he heard the sound of approaching foot-steps and could see the figure of the man he expected.

The approaching knight was Alonso de Carrillo, who, because of the position of honor that he held with the king, had been employed in the royal chamber until that hour. The man who stepped out of the shadows to meet him was Lope de Sandoval. When they faced each other, the two knights exchanged a few quiet words. One said, "I thought that you would be expecting me." The other answered, "I hoped that you would surmise as much. Where shall we go?" The first knight replied, "Wherever we can find enough room to turn around in and sufficient light."

The two young men walked down one of the narrow streets leading from the Zocodover and continued on through the dark streets of Toledo. In fact, the night was so dark that a duel did not seem possible. Nevertheless, both knights wanted to fight before the sun came up. The next morning, the royal army was scheduled to move toward the front, and Alonso would go with them. They pressed on through deserted squares and gloomy passageways, until at last they saw a light in the distance that appeared to be surrounded by a ghostly mist.

They had reached the Street of the Christ. The light they saw came from a small lantern that illuminated the image that gives the street its name. They quickened their steps and soon were at the shrine where the lantern burned. An image of the Redeemer, nailed to the cross, with a skull at his feet, was set in an arched recess in a wall covered with ivy.

The cavaliers reverently honored the image of Christ by removing their caps and saying a short prayer. They glanced around, threw off their cloaks, acknowledged their readiness for combat with a nod of the head, and crossed swords. Their blades had hardly touched when the light went out. Neither a step nor a blow had been taken before the street was plunged into total darkness. They stepped backwards and lowered their swords. The light came back on.

Alonso observed that it must have been a gust of wind that lowered the flame. He placed himself on guard and gave warning to Lope, who seemed preoccupied. Lope stepped forward to recover the lost ground and extended his arm so that the mens' blades touched once more. As soon as the blades touched, the light went out again. Lope noted that this was strange, when the two parted and the flame had come back on again. The light spread a radiance over the skull at the feet of Christ.

Alonso said, "Bah! It must be because the holy woman who is in charge of the lamp cheats the worshippers and lets the oil run low, so that the light, almost out, brightens and then darkens in its dying agony." He then placed himself again in a defensive position. His opponent did the same. Then, not only were they enveloped in a thick and impenetrable gloom, but they simultaneously heard the deep echo of a mysterious voice that reminded them of the sighs of a southwest wind in the narrow streets of Toledo.

It is not known what was said by that fearful superhuman voice; however, on hearing it, both youths were seized with terror. They dropped their swords and their hair stood on end. Their bodies were shaken by a tremor, and they broke out in a cold sweat.

The light came on again.

Lope beheld his opponent, who in earlier days had been his best friend, and said, "Ah! God does not mean to permit this combat, for it is a fratricidal contest. A duel between us is an offense to heaven in whose sight we have sworn a hundred times eternal friendship." He threw himself into the arms of Alonso, who clasped him in his own arms with notable strength and fervor. They renewed their friendship.

Alonso said, "Lope, I know that you love Dona Ines, perhaps not as much as I, but you love her. Since a duel between us is impossible, let us place our fate in her hands. Let us go and see her and let her decide which of us shall be happy and which shall be wretched. Her decision shall be respected by both, and he who does not gain her favor tomorrow shall go forth with the King of Toledo and seek diversion in the excitement of war."

Lope agreed, and the friends made their way arm in arm towards the palace near the cathedral, where Dona Ines lived. It was early dawn, and because some of the relatives of Dona Ines were going to march with the Royal Army the next day, it was not possible to gain admittance.

Alonso and Lope heard an unusual noise as they arrived at the base of the Gothic tower of the cathedral, so they stepped into one of the angles where they were concealed by the shadows of the buttresses. To their amazement, they saw a man emerging from a window of the balcony of the apartment of Dona Ines. He climbed down to the ground with the help of a rope and looked up at a white figure, Dona Ines, leaning over the parapet to exchange tender words of farewell with her mysterious lover.

The first reaction of the youths was to place their hands on their sword hilts, until they turned toward each other and noted the look of astonishment on each other's face. The situation was so ludicrous that they broke out into loud laughter that echoed from the buildings, resounding into the square and even to the palace. Hearing it, the figure in white vanished from the balcony.

The next day, the queen, sitting on her sumptuous dais, watched the Royal Army march by on their way to fight the Moors. The ladies of Toledo were at her side, including Dona Ines de Tordesillas, on whom all eyes were cast. However, those looking at her seemed to have a different expression than the one to which she was accustomed. To her, it seemed that in the curious looks cast upon her lurked mocking smiles.

This troubled Dona Ines, because she remembered the laughter that she had heard while standing on her balcony saying goodbye to her lover. As she watched the army march by in their shining armor, she noted the reunited banners of the houses of Carrillo and Sandoval. When, after the former rivals saluted the queen, she saw their taunting smiles directed toward her, she understood it all. She blushed in shame, and tears glistened in her eyes.

Moral: Sometimes we are fortunate that events we want to
      happen do not occur.

Based on: Gustavo Adolfo Becquer, "The Christ of the Skull,"
     Romantic Legends of Spain

David and Goliath

Jesse, who lived long ago in Bethlehem, had eight strong, resolute sons. His youngest son was David. As a boy, David was strong and healthy with a pleasing appearance. When his older brothers drove the sheep to the fields, he went with them. David loved the outdoors and ran around the hillsides listening to the rippling water in the brooks and the songs of birds perched in the trees. He made up songs about the beautiful things that he saw and heard. He was happy and grew in strength.

David did not lack courage. His eyes were sharp and his aim was sure. When he placed a stone in his sling, he never missed his target. As he grew older, he was given the responsibility of tending part of the flock of sheep. One day as he watched his sheep from the hillside, a lion dashed out of the nearby woods and seized a lamb. David leaped to his feet and ran toward the lion without hesitating.

David had no fear; he just wanted to save the lamb that he was responsible for. He jumped on the lion, seized his head, and, with his wooden staff as his only weapon, slew him. Another day, a bear came out of the woods and approached the flock. David killed the bear also.

Soon after these events, the Philistines assembled an army and

109

marched over the hills to drive the people of Israel from their homes. King Saul marshaled the Israelite army and went out to meet his enemies. David's three oldest brothers joined King Saul's army, but David was left at home to tend the sheep. His brothers told him that he was too young to fight; besides, someone had to protect the flocks.

Forty days passed and no word was received from King Saul's army. Jesse asked David to go to the encampment to take food to his brothers and see how they were doing. David traveled to the hill on which King Saul's army was camped. He heard much shouting and saw that the armies were formed to do battle. David walked through the ranks and finally found his brothers. As he stood talking with them, the shouting stopped, and the armies became very quiet.

David saw that a giant stood on the opposite hillside. As the giant paced up and down, his armor glistened in the sun. His sword and shield were so heavy that none of King Saul's men could have lifted them. David's brothers said that this was the great giant, Goliath. Every day, he walked towards them and called out challenges to the men of Israel. No one in the Israelite army dared to take him on.

David was astounded; he wondered if the men of Israel were afraid. He asked how they could let this Philistine defy the army of Israel. Was no one willing to go out and meet him? Eliab, David's oldest brother, grew angry and accused his brother of being haughty and proud. He jeered that David had come merely to watch a battle, and that he should be at home tending the sheep. David told Eliab that the keeper was tending the sheep, and that their father had asked him to come. He added that he was glad that he had come, because he was going to take on the giant.

David said that he had no fear of the giant because the God of Israel was with him. Some men standing nearby told King Saul of David's willingness to fight Goliath. King Saul asked them to bring David to him. When the king saw how young David was, he tried to discourage him. David told King Saul how he had killed the lion and the bear with his bare hands and a staff. David said that the good Lord had delivered him from them and would also deliver him from the hands of this oversized Philistine.

King Saul told David to undertake his task and prayed that the

Lord would go with him. The king offered David the use of his sword, coat of mail, and helmet. David refused them, admitting that he was not skilled in their use. He knew that a man must win his battles on his own terms and with his own weapons.

David left the encampment with just his staff, his shepherd's bag, and his sling. He ran down to the brook at the foot of the hill. He leaned down and picked up five smooth stones from the brook and dropped them into his bag. The great giant stalked toward David while the men of both armies looked on in awe from the hillsides.

When the giant saw saw how young David was, he was angry. He thought the men of Israel were mocking him by sending one so young against him. Goliath asked if the youth considered him a dog to be attacked by sticks. He told David to turn back or he would feed his flesh to the beasts of the field and the birds of the air. Then the giant cursed David in the name of all of his gods.

David was still without fear. He called out that Goliath came to fight with a sword, a spear, and a shield, but that he came in the name of the Lord, the God of the army of Israel, whom the Philistines had defied. He told the giant that the Lord would deliver him into his hands and defeat him, and all would know about the God of Israel.

The giant ran toward David, and David advanced even faster toward the giant. David reached into his bag for a stone and loaded it into his sling. His keen eye found the place in the Giant's forehead where the helmet joined. He drew his sling, and, with all the force of his strong right arm, hurled the stone. The stone whizzed through the air and struck deep into the vulnerable place in Goliath's forehead. His huge body tottered and then toppled to the ground. As Goliath lay with his face toward the ground, David ran quickly to his side, drew the giant's sword, and severed his head from his body.

When the army of Israel saw this, they shouted and ran down the hillside toward the Philistine army. As the Philistines realized that their greatest warrior had been slain by a young man, they fled, leaving their tents and all their belongings as spoils for the men of Israel.

At the conclusion of the battle, King Saul asked for the young victor to be brought before him. He asked David to stay with him as his own son instead of returning to Jesse's house. David stayed with King Saul and eventually was given command of the army of Israel. All Israel honored him. Years later, when Saul stepped down as king, David succeeded him.

Moral: Courage can overcome what appear to be unsurmountable odds.

Based on: J. Berg Esenwein and Marietta Stockard, "David and Goliath," *Children's Stories and How to Tell Them*

The Legend of Scarface

Among a Blackfoot Indian tribe once lived a poor boy whose father and mother were dead and who had no relatives to take care of him. Kindly women helped him as much as they could. They gave him the food and clothing they could spare and provided shelter during the winter months. The men took him along on hunting expeditions and taught him woodcraft, just as they taught their own sons.

The boy grew up strong and brave, and the men of the tribe said that he would one day make a great hunter. On a hunting party when he was still quite young, he encountered a huge grizzly bear, fought a desperate fight with him, and finally killed him. During the struggle, the bear set its claws in the boy's face and tore it cruelly. An unsightly red mark was left after the wound healed. From then on, he was called Scarface.

The boy was not concerned about his disfigurement until he fell in love with the daughter of the chief of the tribe. His heart ached when he saw all the handsome young braves dressing themselves in the brightly colored attire of the Blackfoot warrior and paying court to the young maiden at her father's wigwam. He knew he could not compete with them for her favor because he was poor and friendless, but particularly because of his scar.

In truth, he maiden did not not care for the other young warriors' finery and boastful talk. Each young man, when he got up the courage to ask for her hand in marriage, was refused. Scarface hesitated to approach her; nevertheless, the girl often saw him as he went about in the forest, and she considered him braver and truer than the young men who sought her favor.

One day as the young woman sat outside her father's lodge, Scarface walked by and looked at her. His eyes showed his love and admiration. A young brave whom the girl had refused noticed this look and sneered, "Scarface has become a suitor for our chief's daughter. She will have nothing to do with men unblemished; perhaps she desires a man marked and marred. Try then, Scarface, and see if she will take you."

Anger rose within Scarface against the young man who had mocked him. He stood proudly, as though he were a chief's son instead of a poor, disfigured warrior. He looked directly at the young brave and said, "My brother speaks true words, although he speaks them with an ill tongue. Indeed, I go to ask the daughter of our great chief to be my wife."

The young brave laughed mockingly. Other young braves joined them, and he told them what Scarface had said. They also laughed, called him the great chief, spoke of his vast wealth and great beauty, and pretended to bow down before him.

Scarface ignored them; he walked away quietly although he yearned to spring at them, as the grizzly had sprung at him in the forest. He went down to the river, following the chief's daughter who had gone to gather rushes for baskets she was weaving. His anger died away and he went up to her, knowing if he did not speak at once his courage would leave him. Although she was gentle and kind, he trembled in her presence as the fiercest warrior or meanest bear could not make him tremble.

Scarface said, "Maiden, I am poor and little thought of, because I have no store of furs or pemmican, as the great warriors of the tribe have. I must gain day by day with my bow and my spear and with hard toil, the means by which I live. My face is marred and unsightly to look upon; however, my heart is full of love for you, and I greatly desire you for my wife. Will you marry me and live with me in my poor lodge?"

She replied, "That you are poor matters little. My father would give me all the things needed for a wedding portion. But I may not be your bride, nor the bride of any man of the tribe. The great Lord of the Sun has laid his commands upon me, forbidding me to marry." Scarface's heart sunk at these terrible words, but he refused to give up hope. He asked, "Will he not release you? He is kind and gives us many gifts. He would not wish to make us both miser-

113

able."

The girl said, "Go to him then and make your prayer to him to set me free from my promise. Ask him that I may know that he has done so by taking the scar off your face as a sign." Scarface told her, "I will go; I will seek out the bright god in his own land and ask him to pity us." He turned away and left the maiden by the river.

Scarface traveled for many miles. Sometimes he was cheerful, saying to himself, "The Sun God is kind; he will give me this bride." At other times, his heart was sad, and he thought, "Maybe the Sun God desires to marry her himself, and who could expect him to give up a maiden so beautiful?" Scarface hiked through forests and over mountains, searching for the golden gates that marked the entrance to the country of the great god.

The wild animals knew that Scarface had not come to hunt them, so they drew willingly around him and answered his questions. Unfortunately, none of them could tell him how to get to the Sun God's land. They told him that they had never traveled beyond the forest. They suggested that he ask the birds, since they fly great distances. Scarface called to the birds flying overhead, and they came down to listen to his question. They were not helpful: "We fly far and see many things, but we have never seen two gleaming gates of gold, nor looked into the face of the bright God of the Sun."

Scarface was disappointed, but he trudged onward. One day when he was very tired, he met a wolverine and asked the question he had asked so many times. He was overjoyed when the wolverine answered, "I have seen the gleaming gates and have entered the bright country of the Lord of the Sun. But the way to it is long and hard, and you will be exhausted when you reach the end of your journey. I will start you on your way; if your heart does not fail you, someday you will see what I have seen." Scarface continued on with renewed courage, day after day. He walked until he was weary, resting infrequently.

One day, Scarface came to a great water that was so broad and deep he could not cross it. It seemed that all of his labor had been for nothing. He sat down on the shore of the great water and felt hope dying in his heart. He looked up and saw two beautiful swans coming toward him from the other side of the water. They said,

"We will take you across. Step on our backs, and we will swim with you to the farther shore." Scarface was joyful again as he poised himself carefully on the backs of the swans. They glided across the water and landed him safely on the opposite shore.

The swans asked him, "Do you seek the kingdom of the Sun God? Go then along the road that lies before you, and you will soon come to it." Scarface thanked them with all of his heart. He walked with quick, light steps. He had not gone far when he saw a beautiful bow and arrows lying on the ground. He stopped to look at them, thinking, "These belong to a mighty hunter; they are finer than those of a common warrior." He left them lying where he found them for, although he coveted them, he was honest and would not take what was not his.

Scarface went on, even lighter of heart than before, and soon he saw a handsome youth coming down the road toward him. It seemed to him that a soft, bright light shone around the youth, who stopped and asked, "I have lost a bow and arrows somewhere along the road. Have you seen them?" Scarface answered, "They lie but a little distance behind me. I have just passed them." The youth said, "Thank you many times. It is well for me that it was an honest man who passed or I should never have seen my bow and arrows again."

He smiled at Scarface, who felt a great joy in his heart; the air seemed flecked with golden points of light. The youth asked, "Where are you going?" Scarface answered, "I seek the land of the great Lord of the Sun, which I believe is very near." The youth replied, "It is near indeed. I am Apisirahts, the Morning Star, and the Sun is my father. Come and I will take you to him."

The two young men walked down the broad, bright road and passed through golden gates. Inside they saw a great lodge, shining and gaily decorated with the most beautiful pictures and carvings Scarface had ever seen. At the door stood a woman with a fair face and bright, clear eyes that looked kindly at the weary stranger. She said, "Come in, I am Kokomikis, the Moon Goddess, and this youth is my son. Come in, for you are tired and footsore and need food and rest."

Scarface, overwhelmed by the beauty of everything around him, went in, and Kokomikis cared for him tenderly. Soon he felt refreshed and strong. Later, the great Lord of the Sun returned to the lodge, and he, too, was very kind to Scarface. He said, "Stay with us. You have traveled a long way to find me; now be my guest for a season. You are a great hunter, and you will find good game here. My son who loves the chase will go with you, and you will live with us and be happy."

Scarface replied that he would stay gladly. For many days, he lived with the Sun God, Kokomikis, and Apisirahts, and every day he and Morning Star went hunting and returned in the evening to the shining lodge. The Lord of the Sun warned them: "Do not go near the great water. Savage birds live there; they will try to slay Morning Star."

Apisirahts secretly longed to take on these savage birds and kill them. One day, he stole away from Scarface and headed for the great water. Initially, Scarface did not miss him. After a time, he looked around and could not find his companion. He searched anxiously, and a terrible fear came into his heart. He set off as fast as he could toward the haunt of the dreaded birds.

Scarface heard horrible cries as he hurried toward the great water. Soon he saw a crowd of the monstrous creatures surrounding Morning Star, pressing him so closely he could not use his weapons to defend himself. Scarface was afraid to shoot an arrow, so he dashed in among the hideous creatures. He took them by surprise, and they flew away in alarm. Then he seized Morning Star and hurried back with him through the forest to safety.

When they returned to the lodge, Apisirahts told his father of his own disobedience and the courage of Scarface. The great Lord of the Sun turned to the poor stranger and said, "You have saved my son from a dreadful death. Ask of me some favor, that I may repay you. Why was it you sought me here? Surely you had some desire in your heart or you would not have traveled so far."

While staying at the shining lodge, Scarface had not forgotten the question he had come there to ask. Many times he had thought, "The hour has come when I may speak," but, because it was such a great favor to ask, his confidence failed him. Each time, he had decided, "I will have patience just a little longer. It is too soon to beg so great a favor of the god who has been so kind to me."

Now when Scarface heard the words of the Sun God, he took courage and replied, "In my own land, oh mighty lord, I love a maiden who is the daughter of the chief of my tribe. I am only a poor warrior, and, as you see, I am disfigured and repulsive to look at. Yet she in her goodness loves me and would marry me, but for the reverence in which she holds your commands laid upon her. For she has promised you, oh great lord, that she will marry no man. So I came to you in hope that you would release her from her promise, that she might come to my lodge and we might live in happiness together."

The Sun God smiled at Scarface, who had spoken bravely while trembling in his heart. The god said, "Go back and take this maiden for your wife. Tell her that it is my will that you marry her, and for a token—he passed his hand across the young suitor's face causing the scar to vanish—tell her to look upon you and see how the God of the Sun has provided the sign of which she spoke."

They loaded the young brave with gifts, and exchanged his poor clothes for the rich dress of an Indian chief. Then they led him out of the country of the Sun, through the golden gates, and showed him an easy path to return to his own land. He traveled quickly and soon was home. The entire tribe came out to look at the richly clad young brave, who walked with a quick, light step and looked so eager and happy. None recognized him as Scarface, whom they had mocked.

At first, even the chief's daughter did not recognize him. A second look told her who he was, and she called his name. When she realized that the scar was gone, she remembered what its disappearance meant and ran toward him with cry of joy. He told the story of his wonderful journey, and the chief gladly gave his daughter to the warrior on whom the great Sun God had looked with favor. They were married that same day, and the chief gave his daughter a splendid wigwam for her marriage portion. They lived happily there for many years. Scarface lost his old name and became known to the tribe as Smoothface.

Moral: Fortitude can overcome many obstacles when it is
accompanied by honesty, loyalty, courage, and
self-discipline.

Based on: Amy Cruse, "The Story of Scarface," *The Book of Myths*

Citizen Soldier Cincinnatus

Lucius Quintius Cincinnatus was one of the heroes of early Rome. He lived outside the city on a farm that he worked with his own hands. Tilling the soil was considered a noble occupation. Cincinnatus was trusted by everyone and considered wise. His advice was frequently sought.

In 458 BC, the Aequians, fierce, half-wild men who lived in the mountains, marched on Rome, stealing and plundering as they came. They threatened to tear down the walls of Rome, burn the houses, kill the men, and make slaves of the women and children. The Romans did not consider themselves in danger because their army, though small, was the finest in the world. The entire army went out to fight the Aequians, leaving only old men, young boys, and a small company of soldiers to guard the walls.

One morning, five horsemen covered with dust and blood came down the road from the mountains as fast as they could ride. The guards on the walls of the city recognized the mounted soldiers and shouted questions. Instead of stopping, however, the soldiers rode to the center of the city to find the older men who had stayed in Rome.

The riders told the city fathers how the Roman army had marched up a narrow valley between two steep mountains. Suddenly a thousand savage men appeared in front of them and above them and threw rocks down on them. The Aequians had blocked the road in front of the army and the path was so narrow that the Romans could not fight. They tried to return the way they had come but were blocked in the rear also. They were trapped.

Ten men spurred their horses and tried to break through. Five made it, but the other five were pierced with spears and died. The five survivors appealed to their elders to send help to their soldiers. Otherwise, they would all perish and the city would be taken. The city fathers shook their heads, not knowing what they could do. Finally, one of them suggested sending for Cincinnatus. He would know what to do. Cincinnatus was plowing one of his fields when the mounted soldiers arrived. They asked him to put on his cloak and come with them to speak with the Roman people. He asked how things were in Rome and was told about the disaster the previous day, and how the army was trapped in a mountain pass. Cincinnatus set his plow aside and went with the soldiers. The men told him that the people of Rome wanted him to be their ruler and to govern the city. As he rode through the city streets, he issued orders about what must be done.

Cincinnatus armed the boys and the company of men guarding the wall and marched out to engage the mountain men. In one day, he freed the trapped army in the narrow pass and defeated the Aequians, driving them back into the mountains. Then, with banners flying and shouts of victory, Cincinnatus led the Roman army, the guards, and the boys back to the city. He had saved Rome. He could have proclaimed himself king, but he ruled briefly and then returned power to the city fathers and went back to his farm.

Moral: When called upon to serve your country, give the help that is needed even if it means putting yourself in harm's way.

Based on: James Baldwin, "The Story of Cincinnatus," *Favorite Tales of Long Ago*

The Legend of Roland

The legend of Roland is based upon *La Chanson de Roland*, the finest epic poem among eighty epics composed in French. This work of an unknown author (c. 1100) belongs to a cycle of epics centered around the life of Charlemagne. Religious fervor was at its height at the beginning of the crusading era in the eleventh century. The first crusade of 1096-1099 was preceded by a number of expeditions against the Arabs in Spain. In the legend of Roland, Charlemagne invaded Spain as the champion of Christianity against the Saracens, with his rear guard forced to fight a courageous battle against vastly superior forces.

Charlemagne had subdued all of Spain except for Saragossa and its Saracen king, Marsile, after seven years of campaigning. Hard-pressed, Marsile assembled his dukes and counts and sought their counsel. Only one, Blancandrin, offered advice: Marsile should follow Charlemagne to his capital, Aix-la-Chapelle, and promise to become a Christian. This promise, which Marsile did not intend to keep, would induce Charlemagne to leave Spain. Marsile asked Blancandrin to lead a delegation to Charlemagne.

Charlemagne was resting in a orchard with his nephew Roland,

Olivier, and other leaders of his army. Roland told the Emperor that the Arabs were treacherous and not to be trusted. However, Roland's stepfather Ganelon argued for accepting the Arab offer, and Charlemagne agreed.

An emissary to Marsile was needed. Roland volunteered, but his friend Olivier said that he was too impetuous. Olivier offered to go, but Charlemagne would not permit any of his twelve peers, the elite of his army, to go on so dangerous a mission. Roland suggested that Ganelon go, emphasizing his inferiority to the twelve peers. Ganelon had no grounds on which to refuse. Furious, he said that if he returned he would take revenge. Roland taunted him even more by offering to take his place. In his agitation, Ganelon dropped the glove, the symbol of his office as Charlemagne's emissary. The French interpreted this as a bad omen.

Ganelon plotted Roland's death while riding to the Saracen camp with Blancandrin. The Arabs would attack the rear guard, which would be commanded by Roland and Olivier. With Roland dead, Charlemagne would lose the desire to wage war. The plot was agreed upon in the Saracen camp.

Ganelon returned to Charlemagne's headquarters, and the French prepared to leave for home. The Arabs took up position to ambush the rear guard. Charlemagne dreamed of impending disaster. The next day, when he asked his barons to appoint commanders for the rear guard, Ganelon immediately proposed Roland, who could not refuse. The Emperor, suspecting treachery, offered Roland half the army, but Roland proudly declined.

The French army began its march homeward through the passes of the Pyrenees, leaving only the rearguard in Spain. The Saracens prepared to attack. Olivier saw them approaching, and three times urged Roland to recall the main army while there was still time. Roland was too proud to do it:

> "Companion Roland, pray sound your horn!
> Charles will hear it and turn back the army."
> Roland replies: "I should be acting like a madman,
> In sweet France, I should lose my reputation..."

> "Companion Roland, pray sound the olifant [horn],
> Charles will hear it and turn back the army.

The king will come to our assistance with his barons."
Roland replies: "May God forbid
That my relatives should be blamed on my account
Or sweet France disgraced..."

"Companion Roland, sound your olifant,
Charles will hear it as he goes through the passes,
I promise you, the Franks will at once turn back."
"God forbid," replies Roland,
"That it be said by any man
That I blew my horn because of a pagan!
Never shall my relatives suffer the reproach..."

Thus the Battle of Rencesvals began, with Roland striking the first blow. Gradually, the Arabs' superior numbers told. A raging storm hung over France and darkness fell at noon, foretelling Roland's death. The rear guard was cut down down until only sixty men were left. Roland finally decided to recall Charlemagne. Olivier objected because it was then too late. He taunted Roland about his earlier remarks about disgracing his relatives.

Olivier told Roland, "All this carnage is your fault! You out-stretched yourself today. If you had listened when I spoke, Charlemagne would be here now. You have lost us by your pride, Roland! Before evening, you and I will say farewell."

Blowing the horn with all his might, Roland burst a blood vessel in his temple, which would be the eventual cause of his death. The blast of his horn could be heard for a great distance. Hearing it, Charlemagne decided to return at once, but it was too late. Olivier was killed, and at the end, only Bishop Turpin and Roland remained alive. Bishop Turpin attempted to obtain water for Roland but collapsed and died. Roland, after trying unsuccessfully to shatter his great sword, Durendal, on the rocks, placed it and the horn beneath him, his face turned toward the Saracen army. Aware that the French are returning, the Saracen army decided to with-draw. Roland died, and angels bore his soul up to heaven.

Arriving at the scene of the massacre, Charlemagne and his men mourned the loss of the rear guard. The French pursued the Arabs towards Saragossa. God held the setting sun in the sky. Many Arabs were killed by the sword, and many were drowned trying to cross the swiftly flowing Ebro River. Charlemagne knelt and gave thanks to God. When he rose, the sun had set.

Large Saracen forces under the command of Emir Baligant came to Marsile's aid, and a new battle began. Charlemagne and Baligant fought hand-to-hand, and the Emperor, with the encouragement of the angel Gabriel ringing in his ears, was victorious. The Arabs, after having lost their leader, took flight, and Charlemagne occupied Saragossa. The French returned home. On hearing of Roland's death, Alde, Olivier's sister, fell dead at Charlemagne's feet.

The traitor Ganelon was tried and sentenced to death. Charlemagne lamented on hearing from the angel Gabriel that his troubles were not over.

Moral: Pride should not be allowed to stand in the way of reason.

Based on: Norma Lorre Goodrich, "Roland at Rencesvals,"
　　　　　Myths of the Hero, and Richard Cavendish, "The Song
　　　　　of Roland," *Legends of the World*

Chapter 7

EMPATHETIC / COMPASSIONATE

A man to be greatly good,
Must imagine intensely and comprehensively;
He must put himself in the place of another and many others;
The pains and pleasures of his species must become his own.

Percy Bysshe Shelly, *A Defence of Poetry*

Where Love Is, God Is

Martin Avdeich, a shoemaker, had lived in a small town for a long time and had many friends. He lived in a basement room with one window looking out onto the street. Through it, he could see the feet of those passing by. Martin could tell who they were from their shoes. There were few pairs of shoes in the neighborhood that had not passed through his hands once or twice. Some he had resoled, others he had put on new heels, still others he had stitched up. He could see the results of his handiwork through the window.

Martin was always busy, since he did excellent work, used quality materials, never overcharged, and was reliable. If he knew he could complete a job on time, he took on the job. If not, he would not make false promises to his customers. Everyone knew Martin, and he was never short of work. He had always been a good man, and he became closer to God as he grew older.

Martin's wife died while he was still an apprentice, leaving him with a three-year-old son. None of their other children survived infancy. Initially Martin considered sending his son to stay with his sister in the country, but he decided against parting with him. He did not want his little son to grow up in a strange family, so he kept little Kapiton with him.

However, it was not God's wish for Martin to find happiness in his children. As soon as Kapiton had grown up and was able to help his father and bring him joy, he became ill and died. After Martin had buried his son, he became despondent and blamed God for everything. He was so overcome by grief that he begged God to let him die. He reproached Him for taking his beloved son instead of an old man like him. He stopped going to church.

A wise old man from the same village as Martin, who had been wandering around the countryside for eight years, called to see him on his way back from the Monastery of the Holy Trinity. Martin opened his heart to him, bemoaning his sad lot: "Holy man, I've lost the will to live. All I want to do is die; that's all I ask of God. There is nothing left for me now."

The holy man told him: "It is wicked to talk like that, Martin. It is not for us to question the ways of God. We must bow to God's judgment and not always be guided by our own reason. If it was God's will that your son should die and you should live, then it must be for the best. You are in despair because you only want to live for your own happiness." Martin asked what else he should live for.

The old man replied, "You must live for God, Martin. He gave you life, so it is Him you should live for. If you live for Him, you will never grieve again, and all your sorrows will be easy to bear." Martin asked how one should live for God. The old man answered, "It was Christ who showed us how to live for God. Can you read? Well, go and buy the Gospels and study them. Then you will discover how to live for God. Everything is written there."

These words made a strong impression on Martin. He bought a copy of the New Testament and sat down to read. At first, he intended to read the Gospels only on church holidays, but, once he began to read, he was so uplifted that he read them every day. Sometimes he became so engrossed that he stopped reading only when the lamp ran out of oil. He read every evening. The more he read, the more clearly he understood what God required of him, and how he could live for Him.

Consequently, Martin's heart grew lighter and lighter. Before, when he had gone to bed, he would lie moaning and sighing as he thought of his little son; now he would simply say over and over, "Glory to Thee, oh Lord! Thy will be done." Martin's life was completely transformed.

On church holidays, Martin had been in the habit of going to drink tea at a tavern, and he would never refuse a glass of two of vodka. Although he was never drunk when he left the tavern, he would be somewhat under the influence. He would talk nonsense, shout at his friends, and say nasty things.

Now that became a thing of the past, and his life became peaceful and full of joy. In the morning he would sit down to work. When he had finished, he would take the lamp off its hook, place it on the table, take the Bible from the shelf, and start reading. The more he read, the more he understood, the clearer his mind became, and the happier he was.

One evening Martin sat reading his Bible until very late. He was reading the sixth chapter of St. Luke and came to the following verses:

> And unto him that strikes you on the one cheek offer also the other; and him that take away your cloak forbid not to take your coat also. Give to every man that asks of you; and

125

of him that takes away your goods, ask them not again. And as you would that men should do to you, do you also to them likewise.

He read further, where the Lord says,

> And why call me Lord, and do not the things which I say? Whosoever comes to Me and hears My sayings, and does them, I will show you to whom he is like: he is like a man who built a house, and dug deep, and laid the foundation on a rock; and when the flood rose, the stream beat vehemently upon that house and could not shake it, for it was founded on a rock. But he that hears, and does not, is like a man that without a foundation built a house upon the earth; against which the stream did beat vehemently, and immediately it fell; and the ruin of that house was great.

When Martin read those words, his heart filled with joy. He took off his glasses, placed them on the Bible, leaned his elbows on the table, and pondered for a moment. As he reviewed his own life in the light of those words, he wondered, "Is my house built on a rock or on sand? If it is built on rock, then all is well. It is easy enough, sitting here thinking I have done all that God has commanded. But then I might be tempted to sin again. I shall not give up. Help me, oh Lord!"

After these reflections, he had intended to go to bed, but he could not tear himself away from the Bible. So he began reading the seventh chapter about the centurion, the widow's son, and the answer to John's disciples. He came to the passage where the rich Pharisee invited Christ into his house and where the woman who had sinned anointed His feet and washed them with her tears. Christ had forgiven her. At verse forty-four, he read:

> And He turned to the woman and said to Simon, see you this woman? I entered into your house; you gave me no water for my feet; but she has washed my feet with tears and wiped them with the hairs of her head. You gave me no kiss; but this woman since the time I came in, has not ceased to kiss my feet. My head with oil you did not

anoint; but this woman has anointed my feet with oint-
ment.

Martin took off his glasses again, placed them on the Bible, and
thought hard: "That Pharisee Simon must have been like me. I have
only worried about myself, thinking about the next cup of tea,
keeping warm and cosy, and I have never shown anyone hospitality. Simon only worried about himself and could not have cared less
about his guest. And who was his guest? It was Christ himself.
Would I have behaved like that if Christ had come here?"

Martin laid his head on his arms and fell asleep immediately.
He heard his name called, as though someone were whispering into
his ear. He was startled and asked sleepily, "Who's there? He turned
around and looked toward the door—no one was there. He laid his
head down again to sleep and heard quite distinctly, "Martin!
Martin! Look out into the street tomorrow, for I will come."

Martin roused himself, got up from the chair, and rubbed his
eyes. He did not know if he had been dreaming or awake when he
heard those words. He put out the lamp and went to bed. The next
morning Martin got up before dawn and said his prayers. He lit the
stove, warmed up some porridge, lit the samovar, and sat down to
work by the window. However, he could not forget what had happened the evening before. On one hand, he wondered if he had
imagined everything; on the other, he persuaded himself that it had
happened. He decided that he really did hear a voice.

As Martin sat at his window, he concentrated more on what was
happening outside than on his work. Whenever anyone walked by
in unfamiliar boots, he would strain to see the person's face as well
as their feet. A porter went by in felt boots, then a water carrier.
Next to walk by was an old soldier wearing patched felt boots and
carrying a shovel.

Martin recognized him from the boots. His name was
Stepanych; a neighboring tradesman gave him food and lodging out
of charity. His job was to help the porter. He began clearing the
snow outside Martin's window. Martin resumed work and thought,
"I must be going soft in the head! It is only old Stepanych clearing
away the snow, and I immediately think that it is Christ who has
come to visit me."

After a dozen more stitches, Martin again felt the urge to look out of the window. This time he saw that Stepanych had propped his shovel against the wall. Martin could not see whether he was warming himself or simply resting. Obviously, he was only a poor, broken-down man who just did not have the strength to clear the snow away. Martin decided to offer him a cup of tea, particularly since the samovar was on the boil. He put the samovar on the table, made tea, and tapped on the window. Stepanych turned around and came to the window. Martin motioned for him to come inside and went to open the door.

Martin said, "Come inside and warm yourself. You must be frozen stiff." Stepanych replied, "God bless you! My bones are aching." He came inside, shook off the snow, and wiped his feet so as not to dirty the floor. Martin invited him to sit down and offered him tea. He filled two glasses and offered one to his guest. When Stepanych finished his tea, he turned his glass upside down and thanked his host. It was obvious that he wanted some more. Martin refilled the two glasses and told Stepanych to drink up.

As Martin drank his tea, he kept looking out into the street. His guest asked if he were expecting someone. Martin replied, "Am I expecting someone? I feel ashamed to tell you. As it happens, I am both expecting and not expecting. The fact is, there are some things I cannot get out of my head. Whether I imagined I heard them, I really can't say. Last night I was reading the Gospels, about our dear Lord and how He suffered and walked this earth. I'm sure you must have heard about it." Stepanych said, "Yes, I've heard about it; but I'm an ignorant man and can't read or write."

Martin explained: "I was reading about how He walked this earth and how He went to the house of Simon the Pharisee, who did not make Him welcome. As I read further, I thought to myself how badly Christ was treated. Supposing Christ had come to my house, or to someone like me. What wouldn't I have done to give Him a proper welcome. But Simon would not receive Him into his house.

"That's what I was thinking when I fell asleep. In my sleep, I heard someone call my name. When I lifted my head, I thought I could hear someone whispering, 'Expect me, for I shall come and see you tomorrow.' Twice I heard that voice whisper. As you can imagine, those words affected me deeply. I know I'm being silly, but I'm expecting to hear from the Lord."

Stepanych silently shook his head, emptied his glass, and laid it on its side. Martin stood it up again, refilled it, and said, "Here, drink some more. I was thinking about the time when our Lord was upon this earth, despising no one and associating mainly with ordinary folks. He spent time with the humble and chose his disciples mainly from folks like us, from ordinary sinners and working people. 'Whosoever exalts himself,' He said, 'The same shall be humbled; and whoever shall humble himself, the same shall be exalted. You call me Lord,' He said, 'but I shall wash your feet. He who would be first, let him be the servant of all. Because,' He said, 'blessed are the poor, the humble, the meek, and the merciful.'"

Stepanych set aside his tea. He was an old man easily moved to tears. As he sat there listening, tears rolled down his cheeks. Martin said, "Come, drink your tea." But Stepanych made a sign of the Cross, thanked him, moved the glass away, and got up. He said, "Thank you, Martin, you have welcomed me and nourished me in spirit and body." Martin told him, "You are always welcome here. I'm only too glad to have a visitor."

Stepanych left, and Martin poured out what was left of the tea, drank it, cleared the glasses away, sat down by the window, and began stitching the back of a shoe. As he stitched, he kept looking out of the window, waiting for Christ and thinking only of Him and His works. His head was full of Christ's many sayings.

Two soldiers went by: one in army boots, one in his own; then the owner of the house next door in galoshes; then a baker with a basket. Then a woman in woolen stockings and rough peasant shoes came towards the window. She stopped by the wall. Martin looked up at her from the window and saw that she was a stranger, poorly dressed, and that she held a child in her arms. She was wearing a shabby summer dress and stood against the wall with her back to the wind. She tried to wrap the baby up; unfortunately, she had nothing much to wrap it in.

Martin could hear the baby crying. He got up, went to the door, climbed the steps, and called out, "My dear woman!" She heard him and turned around. He asked, "Why are you standing out there in the freezing cold? And with a little child! Come inside, you can make him nice and warm in here. Follow me." The woman was surprised to see and old man in an apron, with glasses on his nose, calling out to her. She followed him down the stairs into the little room, where he led her to sit by the stove. He suggested that she warm herself and feed the baby. She mentioned that she hadn't eaten anything yet that day, and that she had no milk.

Martin went to get some bread and a bowl, into which he poured cabbage soup. He said, "Please sit down and have something to eat, while I hold the baby. I had children of my own once, so I know how to take care of them." The woman sat down, made a sign of the cross, and began to eat, while Martin held the baby. He tried making a smacking sound with his lips to soothe the child, but the baby would not stop crying. He wagged his finger at the baby. The baby stopped crying when he saw the finger blackened with shoe polish and began to laugh. Martin was delighted.

As she ate her soup, the woman told him: "I'm a soldier's wife. They sent my husband far away about eight months ago, and I've heard nothing from him since. I was a cook until my son was born, and then they wouldn't keep me any more. I've been struggling without a job for about three months now. I spent all the money I had on food. I wanted to become a wet nurse but no one would take me; they said I was too thin.

"I've just been to see a tradesman's wife. A woman from our village works for her; she promised to employ me, but now she tells me to come back next week. She lives a long way from here. I'm worn out and my baby's cold and hungry. Thank God my landlady has taken pity on us and given us free lodging. Otherwise, I wouldn't know what to do."

Martin asked her if she had anything warmer to wear. She told him that she had to pawn her shawl for a few kopecks. The woman finished eating and went over and took the child from Martin. He stood up and went over and rummaged about until he found an old jacket. He handed it to her to wrap around the baby. She looked at the jacket, then at the old man, and burst into tears as she took it. Martin turned away and went to look for more clothing, without success.

The woman said, "May the Lord bless you! It must have been Christ Himself who sent me to your window; otherwise my baby would have perished from the cold. When I started out this morning, it was mild, but now it is freezing. It must have been Christ who encouraged you to look out of your window and take pity on a poor wretch like me."

Martin smiled and said, "You are right. It was He who encouraged me, and I had good reason, my dear!" Martin told the soldier's wife about his dream, and how he had heard a voice promising him that the Lord would visit him that day. "Yes, all things are possible," the woman said, getting up. She threw the jacket over herself and the baby, curtseyed, and thanked Martin again. He handed her a twenty-kopeck note to get her shawl out of the pawnshop. The woman crossed herself, and so did Martin as he saw her out.

After the woman had left, Martin had some soup, cleared the table, and sat down to work. As he worked, he continued to watch the window. Every time a shadow would fall across it, he would immediately look up to see who was passing. People he knew and strangers passed, but no one in particular.

Then an old market woman stopped right in front of his window. She was carrying an apple basket but appeared to have sold most of her wares, since it was almost empty. On one shoulder was a sack of wood shavings that she must have collected at a building site along the way home. The heavy sack was obviously hurting her. She placed the apple basket on a post and put the sack down on the pavement to shift it to her other shoulder. As she was doing this, a boy in a ragged cap suddenly ran up and grabbed an apple from her basket and tried to run off with it.

The old woman had seen him coming and turned to grab his sleeve. The boy struggled to get free, but the woman seized him with both hands, knocked off his cap, and held him by his hair. The boy screamed, and the woman cursed. Martin rushed through the doorway and up the stairs. In the street, the woman was cursing away, and evidently intended to haul the boy off to the police station. He struggled and claimed to be innocent.

Martin separated them and said, "Let him go, grandma. Forgive him." She replied, "I'll forgive him but not before he has had the feel of some new birch branches! I'm taking the little devil to the police station." Martin tried to dissuade her and said, "Please let him go, grandma. He won't ever do it again. Let him go."

The old woman released the boy who wanted to run off, but Martin stopped him. Martin told him, "You should ask the old woman to forgive you, and don't ever do it again. I saw you take it." The boy burst into tears and asked her to forgive him. "That's the way! Now, here's an apple for you," Martin said, taking an apple from the basket and handing it to the boy. "I'll pay for it, grandma," he added. She said, "You'll only spoil little devils like him that way. What he deserves is a thrashing so he won't be able to sit down for a week."

Martin exclaimed, "Oh, grandma! That may be our way, but it's not God's way. If the punishment for stealing just one apple is a thorough thrashing, then what would we deserve for our mortal sins?" The old woman did not reply. Martin told her the parable of the master who excused one of his servants a great debt, and how that servant went out and seized his own debtor by the throat. The old woman listened and so did the boy. Martin observed, "God has commanded us to forgive; otherwise, He will not forgive us. We should forgive everyone, even thoughtless little boys."

The old woman shook her head and sighed: "That's all very well, but children are terribly spoiled these days." Martin said, "Then it's up to us to teach them what's right." The old woman replied, "Yes, I agree. I had seven children once, but now I only have one daughter." She told him how and where she and her daughter were living, and how many grandchildren she had. She added: "As you can see, I'm not very strong, but I still have to work myself to the bone. I feel so sorry for my poor grandchildren. No one is as kind to me as they are, and my daughter wouldn't leave me for anyone." The old woman was quite overcome.

Looking at the boy, the woman added, "Well, I suppose it's because he's so young. May God be with him." She was about to lift the sack to her shoulder, when the boy immediately came over to help. He said, "Let me carry that for you, grandma. I am going your way." The old woman accepted his offer and put the sack on his back. As they went down the street, Martin realized that the woman had forgotten to ask him to pay for the apple. He stood there, watching and listening to them as they went.

When they were out of sight, Martin went in and picked up his awl and started working again. Before long, he could no longer see to pass the thread through the holes in the leather. Then he saw the lamplighter on his rounds. He realized that he needed some proper light to work by, so he trimmed the wick of his lamp, hung it up, and got back to work. After finishing one boot, he turned it over to inspect it. It was perfect. He put his tools aside, swept up the cuttings, cleared away the laces and pieces of leather, placed his lamp on the table and took his Gospels from the shelf.

Martin meant to open them at the place that he had marked with a strip of leather the previous day, but the Book fell open at a different page. When he saw it, he remembered last evening's dream. No sooner did he remember it than he heard footsteps, as though someone was there, moving around behind him. Martin turned and saw what appeared to be people in the dark corner, but he could not make out who they were.

A voice whispered in his ear, "Martin! Martin! Don't you know me?" Martin asked, "Who is it?" The voice said, "It is I. Behold, it is I." And Stepanych stepped out of the dark corner. He smiled and then was gone, melting away like a cloud. "It is I," repeated the voice. Our of the dark corner stepped the woman with the baby. She smiled, and so did the child, and then they too vanished. "It is I!" said the voice. Out stepped the old woman and the boy with the apple. Both smiled, and then they too disappeared.

Martin's heart was filled with joy. He crossed himself, put on his glasses, and looked at the page where the Bible had fallen open. He read, "For I was hungry, and you gave Me meat. I was thirsty, and you gave Me drink. I was a stranger and you took Me in ..." And, lower down, "Inasmuch as you have done unto one of the least of My brethren, you have done unto Me" (St. Matthew 25). Martin understood that his dream had come true, that his Savior had visited him that day, and that he had welcomed Him into his house.

Moral: What you have done for the least of God's brethren,
      you have done for Him.

Based on: Leo Tolstoy, "Where Love Is, God Is," *How Much Land Does a Man Need? and Other Stories*

The Legend of Hiawatha

Two Hiawathas have been described: the legendary Hiawatha in "The Song of Hiawatha" by Henry Wadsworth Longfellow and the historical Onondaga Chief who lived near Syracuse, New York, in the fifteenth century. Longfellow's Hiawatha was based on the legendary Indian hero who, as described by Henry Rowe Schoolcraft in *The Myth of Hiawatha*, could take mile-long steps and turn into a wolf. The Hiawatha described by Longfellow could talk with animals and outrun an arrow shot through the air. He was an Ojibwa who lived on the shores of Lake Gitche Gumee near Lake Superior, married Minnehaha, met white people, and became a Christian.

The real Hiawatha lived on the south shore of Cross Lake west of Syracuse during the mid-1400s. He became a leader of the Onondaga Nation, married, and had three (seven in some versions of the story) daughters. His wife's name is lost to history, but it probably was not Minnehaha. Hiawatha's ideas were different from those of his peers; he supported peace, rather than war. The Iroquois Confederacy, which initially included the Senecas, Cayugas, Onondagas, Oneidas, and Mohawks and later added the Tuscaroras, was continually at war—sometimes among themselves but usually with other nations, such as the Hurons from Canada and the Susquehannocks south of them.

Hiawatha was legendary for promoting friendship among the nations at a time when retribution was the policy of the Confederacy. If an Iroquois were killed, the victim's male relatives would kill the murderer. If the murderer could not be found, one of his relatives would be killed in his place. Revenge was a way of life; it did not matter if an innocent person lost his life.

An evil character named Ododarhoh lived south of the principal Onondaga village in a dark ravine near a marsh and slept on a bed of bullrushes. According to legend, the locks of his long, intertwined hair were living snakes. The Onondagas feared him and considered him a wizard. Ododarhoh committed the unspeakable crime of killing Hiawatha's wife and three daughters.

When he heard of their death, Hiawatha threw himself to the ground and thrashed around in anguish. His grief was so deep that people hesitated to approach him and offer their consolation. He left the village, built a lodge of hemlock branches, and became a hermit and an aimless wanderer. Hiawatha was expected to kill Ododarhoh, but it was not his nature to commit an act of revenge, which would never bring back his wife and daughters.

While Hiawatha was in the depths of his despair, he was visited at his lodge by Deganawida the Peacemaker, a Huron evangelist who attempted to convince the Iroquois Confederacy to stop fighting among themselves and to live in peace. He was not having much success; not only because he was an outsider, but also because he stuttered. He was not a good speechmaker. He sought the help of Hiawatha, who was an outstanding speaker respected within the Confederacy.

Hiawatha immediately became a follower of Deganawida. It was too late to protect his own family, but perhaps he could work with the Peacemaker to save the lives of others. Deganawida's ideas brought Hiawatha out of his grief. The Peacemaker's strategy to convince the Onondagas and the other nations of the Confederacy to implement plans for peace was to convert Ododarhoh from his evil ways and to use Hiawatha as the instrument of this conversion. If the Onondagas saw that Hiawatha, upon whom Ododarhoh had inflicted such a terrible loss, could forgive his tormenter and convince him to follow the path of peace, then the rest of the Confederacy would follow.

Deganawida and Hiawatha visited the evil wizard at his lodge in the dark ravine, where Hiawatha placated Ododarhoh by singing to him and speaking a message of peace and Iroquois unity. Ododarhoh's visitors expected him to react violently, because they knew of the evil one's opposition to peace and unity. They expected to be attacked, but Ododarhoh said that he would mend his ways and abide by their proposals. Hiawatha then combed the snakes, which symbolized evil and insane thoughts, out of the wizard's hair. Thus Hiawatha was given the name Ayonwartha, which meant "He who combs."

The Onondaga Nation followed Ododarhoh into the Iroquois Confederacy and the Great Peace. An Onondaga village near Syracuse became the capital of the Confederacy and the location of the council fire. Ododarhoh was named "Firekeeper," a position comparable to President of the Senate. He became one of the most powerful of the sachems. Deganawida and Hiawatha traveled from village to village enlisting support for the Confederacy from the five original Iroquois Nations.

Hiawatha instituted the use of wampum for restitution, rather than taking revenge. Murderers paid for their crimes in wampum, which was frequently made of purple and white shells. Hiawatha was aware that a price could not be set on the value of human life, but it was better for a murderer to pay the victim's family in wampum than to continue a progression of retaliatory killings. Wampum would carry a message as well as have intrinsic value.

When Deganawida saw that his objectives had been accomplished, he said, "Now I shall be seen no more, and I go where none can follow me." Five years after he had arrived among the Onondagas, the Peacemaker climbed into a white birchbark canoe on the eastern shore of Onondaga Lake and paddled westward into the sunset.

Hiawatha, who watched from the shore, continued the work of Deganawida. Historians know little about Hiawatha's later life. Mohawks claim that he lived among them as an elder statesman who cleared rocks and brush from rivers to make them more navigable and to facilitate communications among the villages.

According to Indian legend, Hiawatha left the Iroquois in the same manner that his mentor, Deganawida, did—paddling a white birchbark canoe westward across a lake. The two men were thought to have found happiness in the Sky World, where strawberries grow as large as apples and flowers of white light always bloom. Hiawatha and the Peacemaker had a lasting influence on the Iroquois Confederacy, which for centuries was the most advanced culture in North America.

Moral: No satisfaction is gained from revenge.

Emerson Klees, "The Legend of Hiawatha," *Legends and Stories*

The Treasure of the Muleteer

Some people have a tendency to be overly curious, which causes problems. Centuries ago in Spain, a muleteer from Sobrado del Obisbo lost a fortune due to his wife's curiosity and gossip.

Many years ago, the beautiful land of Galicia was inhabited by Spaniards and by Moors, who had come to Spain from Africa. Moors accomplished great things in Spain, including the construction of castros, concentric circles of rough boulders on virtually inaccessible hilltops. However, not everyone believed that the castros were built by the Moors centuries before.

One who did believe it was a muleteer from Sobrado del Obisbo who carted wine to the outlying villages in his large, creaking cart. He wore down the tracks of the road between his village and Orense, carrying wineskins filled with vintage wine to customers in that city, which was the seat of the Bishop. The muleteer's most important customers were Moors. Regularly, he went to a wine vault, filled his wineskins with the best wine of Ribeiro, and headed down the road to Orense.

After entering the city, the muleteer would lead his mule-drawn cart up the hill to the Castros de Trelles, two outcroppings that blocked the view of the city all the way to the Portuguese border. The Moors waited for him there. They came up from underground where they occupied the many corridors and passages with which they had mined the entire region. Only two entrances existed to these passages, one to the east and another to the west. Moors swarmed out, unloaded the wineskins brought by the muleteer, and in payment gave him fragments of shale they had mined.

The muleteer stored the small chunks of gray rock in his pouch, and when he arrived back home and emptied the pouch, the chips of slate had turned into gold pieces. Eventually, he made these trips to the Castros de Trelles every day. As a consequence, his fortune grew rapidly.

The muleteer's wife, who was very nosy, began to wonder at this strange phenomenon. He formerly had difficulty selling his merchandise even after traveling all over the territory. Now, every day he came back with a purse full of gold pieces. As might be expected, she asked her husband about the source of all that money. The muleteer from Sobrado could not answer, because the Moors had made him swear to tell no one. He either remained quiet or changed the subject when his wife asked.

The muleteer asked his wife if she was satisfied with the pig and the heifer she had bought at the market in Barbantes. He asked her why she should care how he had earned the money. Nevertheless, she kept after him, again, and again, and again. She said that he must tell her, because husbands should have no secrets from their wives. She quizzed him every hour, constantly: morning, afternoon, and night. She kept saying, "You have to tell me."

The muleteer could not stay a moment at home without being bombarded with the same question. Finally, he realized that he had two choices: he could either leave home or reveal the secret to his wife. In a moment of weakness, he chose the latter alternative, imposing many precautions upon her. When the village was asleep, he led her to the farthest corner of the house and told her what was happening. He told her to be careful and tell no one.

The muleteer's wife wife told him it was nonsense to be concerned that she would talk, as quiet and discreet as she was. The isolated rocky peaks of the Monte das Cantarinas or the stone angels over the doorway of the Church of Gloria would talk before anyone would get the Moors' secret out of her.

The following morning, after the muleteer had loaded his cart and headed for the Castros de Trelles, his wife went over to her friend Mariquina's house and whispered what she had learned. Then she went to Carmina's stable and to the Carboeiras' grocery store and chattered some more. She told everyone that her husband was the one who delivered wine to the Moors but not to tell anyone—no one.

When Mariquina, Carmina, and la Carboeira saw their husbands, they scolded them for working all day every day to earn four coppers that bought very little while the muleteer came home with a pouch full of gold. They told their husbands to do what the muleteer did: sell things to the Moors—yes, the Moors.

The muleteer arrived at the Castros de Trelles that day, his wineskins full of good Ribeiro. He waited in vain for his customers to appear. The eastern entrance and the western entrance both stayed tightly shut. He could only return home as though nothing had happened. His neighbors in Sobrado del Obisbo peeked out of their windows as he passed. The natives of Galicia are tough when luck turns her face away from them. He passed by with a grim look on his face and appeared to be muttering under his breath.

The muleteer's wife came out to greet him and told him that she had not said anything to anybody. He glared at her, knowing that she had. He was so angry that he considered striking her, but he controlled himself. Luck had left them, for good. He could not re-establish his relationship with the Moors. The penalty that his wife paid for her loose tongue was to go back to the poverty they had known before her husband began selling wine to the Moors.

Moral: If you give your word, keep it.

Based on: Antonio Jiminez-Landi, "The Treasure of the Muleteer," *The Treasure of the Muleteer and Other Spanish Tales*

Where Is the Head of the Table?

A man once hosted a feast. He invited many of his fellow towns-folk. Among them was a man of great distinction, a scholar and a sage, but a very modest man who did not like being honored. The host wanted to seat him at the head of the table, as was his due according to custom. Instead, the man chose a place at the foot of the table near the door. Now, when the host, who was an under-standing man, saw him do this he seated his other distinguished guests near him, saying, "My masters, wherever this man sits is the head of the table."

Moral: Practice humility. It is not the place that honors the man, but the man that honors the place.

Based on: Luke 14.7-14, *The Holy Bible*, and Nathan Ausubel, "Where is the Head of the Table?" *A Treasury of Jewish Folklore*

What Men Live By

Years ago in Russia, Semyon, a shoemaker who owned neither land nor a house, lived in a peasant's cottage with his wife and children. He supported them by the work that he could get. His work was cheap but bread was expensive, and the little he earned was spent on food for the family. He and his wife had only one winter coat between them, and it was badly worn. He had been saving for two years to buy sheepskins for a new one.

By autumn, he had accumulated a small sum: the three-ruble note his wife kept in a small wooden box and five rubles and twen-ty kopecks that villagers owed him. One morning he decided to go into the village to buy the skins. He put his wife's padded twill jacket over his shirt and over that, his own cloth coat. After break-fast, he put the three-ruble note in his pocket, cut himself a walking stick, and set off for the village. He thought that with the five rubles one of the villagers owed him plus the three he had, he should have enough to buy the sheepskins.

When the shoemaker reached the village, he stopped at Trifonov's cottage to collect his debt, but the man was out. Trifonov's wife did not have the money; she promised to send her husband over with it by the end of the week. Semyon next called on another peasant who said he was short of cash, and all he could manage was twenty kopecks owed for boot repairs. When the shoemaker tried to buy the skins on credit, the dealer would not trust him. He said, "Bring me the money first, then you can pick whatever skins you like. We all know how hard it is to collect what's owed to us."

The shoemaker did little business that day, except for collecting the twenty kopecks and picking up a pair of felt boots that needed new soles. This depressed the shoemaker. After spending the twenty kopecks on vodka, he set off for home without any skins. Earlier that morning, he had felt a sharp nip in the air, but he warmed up after a few vodkas—despite the lack of a winter coat. As he walked down the road striking clumps of earth with his walking stick, he talked to himself.

The shoemaker said, "I feel quite warm without a coat; I've had only a few drops of vodka, yet I can feel it rushing through every vein in my body. I don't need any sheepskins! I'm going home with all my troubles behind me. That's the sort of man I am! Why should I worry? I can survive without a new coat; I won't need one for ages. Only, the wife won't be too happy.

"It's really rotten when you do a job and the customer strings you along and doesn't pay up. You just wait; if you don't bring me the money, I'll have the shirt off your back. I swear it. It's a bit much, a measly twenty kopecks at a time. What can I do with twenty kopecks? Spend it on drink, that's all. You say you are hard up. Well, what about me? You've a house, cattle, everything, but all I have is on my back. You grow your own corn, while I have to go out and buy mine. Whatever happens, I must spend three rubles a week on bread alone. By the time I get home, there won't be any left, and I'll have to fork out another ruble and a half. So, you'd better pay up."

The shoemaker kept muttering to himself until he approached the wayside chapel near a bend in the road, when something whitish behind the chapel caught his eye. It was growing dark, and he could not tell what it was. He thought to himself that maybe it was a light-colored stone or possibly a cow, but it looked more like a man. He wondered what a man would be doing there.

The shoemaker moved closer and could see that it was a man

sitting there, but he couldn't tell if he were dead or alive. The man was naked and quite motionless and had his back propped against the chapel wall. The shoemaker was terrified and thought, "A man has been murdered, stripped naked, and dumped. If I go any nearer I might get mixed up in all sorts of trouble."

The shoemaker hurried on his way. He walked behind the chapel to avoid looking at the man again. After walking a short distance, he turned around and saw that the man was no longer leaning against the wall but was moving, as though trying to see who he was.

The shoemaker became even more frightened and thought, "Shall I go back or simply continue on? If I go back something terrible might happen. Who knows what kind of man he might be? I'll bet he's up to no good. Besides, he might suddenly jump to his feet and start choking the life out of me; there would be nothing I could do about it. And if he doesn't throttle me, I might have to look after him. How can I help a naked man? I couldn't let him have the shirt off my back. Please God, help me!"

The shoemaker walked faster. He had almost left the chapel when his conscience began to bother him. He stopped in the middle of the road and asked himself: "How could you do such a thing, Semyon? That man might be dying miserably, and you're such a coward you would leave him there to die. Or have you become so rich all of a sudden that you're scared he might steal all of your money? You should be ashamed, Semyon!" He turned around and walked up to the man.

After looking closely, Semyon could see that the man was young and healthy and had no bruises. He was just shivering in the cold and scared. The man leaned forward without looking at Semyon and was apparently too weak to lift his eyes. When Semyon got next to him, he suddenly seemed to awaken as if from a trance. He turned his head, opened his eyes, and looked directly at Semyon. That one look was enough to lessen all Semyon's fears. He threw down the felt boots, undid his belt, laid it over the boots, and took off his cloth coat. He told the man that there was no time to talk—to just put on the clothes he was offering and be quick about it.

Semyon reached under the man's arms and tried to lift him, but he got up without any help. Semyon noticed that his body was slender and clean, and he had no wounds; his face was mild and gentle. Semyon put his coat over his shoulders, but the man could not find the sleeves. Semyon guided his arms into them, pulled on the coat, and fastened it with his belt.

Semyon took off his tattered cap and was going to put it on the man's head but decided, since he himself was bald and the man had long hair, to keep it on. He made the man sit down again while he put the felt boots on his feet and said, "There you are my friend. Stretch your legs a bit and warm yourself. Don't worry, it will all be sorted out later. Now, can you walk?"

The man stood up, looked tenderly at Semyon, but was unable to say one word. Semyon asked, "Why don't you say something? Come on, we can't spend all winter here, we must be on our way. Here, you can lean on my stick if you feel weak. Right, come on!" The man began to walk, effortlessly, without lagging behind. Semyon asked him where he was from. He replied that he wasn't from these parts. Semyon had thought so, because he knew everyone around there.

When Semyon asked how he came to be near the chapel, the man said that he couldn't tell him. When Semyon asked if some men had attacked him, he replied that no one harmed him, but that God had punished him. Semyon agreed that we are all in His hands, and asked the man where he was going. He said that he was going nowhere in particular.

Semyon was surprised. The man did not appear to be a ruffian; he was soft-spoken but revealed nothing about himself. Semyon reflected and told the man: "Anything can happen in the world. All right, come home with me, even if it is a bit out of your way." As Semyon walked down the road, the man kept abreast and did not lag behind. The wind blew and the cold air went under Semyon's shirt. The vodka was beginning to wear off; he was chilled to the bone.

Sniffling as he walked along, Semyon wrapped his wife's jacket tighter around himself and thought, "So much for sheepskins! I go off to buy some, and all I do is come home without even the old coat on my back and with a naked stranger into the bargain! Matryona won't be too pleased about that." The thought of his wife depressed him; however, when he remembered the needy look of the stranger at the chapel, he decided that he was doing the right thing.

Semyon's wife had finished her chores early that day. She had chopped the wood, fetched water, fed the children, and had a bite to eat. Then she had sat around trying to decide whether to bake bread that day or the next. One thick slice was left. She thought if Semyon had had dinner in the village, he wouldn't need much supper, and there would be enough bread for tomorrow. She looked at the slice of bread and decided not to bake that day. She knew there was only enough flour for one loaf, and they should be able to make that last until the end of the week.

Matryona put the bread away and sat down at the table to patch her husband's shirt. As she sewed, she thought about Semyon buying sheepskins for the new winter coat; she hoped the dealer wouldn't swindle him. She considered her husband an uncomplicated person; he would never cheat anyone, but even a child could trick him. She thought: "Eight rubles is a lot of money, enough to buy good sheepskins. Last winter was hard without a proper coat. I couldn't go down to the river, couldn't go anywhere. When he left this morning, he took all the warm clothes we have, leaving none for me. It's time that he was back. I hope my old man hasn't been drinking."

Just then, the front steps creaked, and someone came in. She put down her sewing, went into the hall, and saw two men: Semyon and someone in felt boots without a cap. She immediately smelled vodka on her husband's breath. When she saw him standing there, empty-handed with a guilty grin on his face, wearing nothing but the jacket she had lent him, her heart sank. She thought, "So, I was right, he's been drinking. He has spent all that money drinking with some good-for-nothing. He even had the nerve to bring him home."

Matryona followed them into the living room. She saw that the stranger was a thin young man, and that he was wearing her husband's coat. She could see no shirt under it, and he had no cap. The stranger stood still and kept looking down. He seemed so nervous; she concluded that he was a bad lot. Frowning, she went over to the stove to see what they would do next. Semyon removed his cap, sat down on the bench as if he had done nothing wrong, and asked Matryona for some supper.

Matryona muttered something to herself, looking first at one and then at the other. Semyon realized that his wife was annoyed, but he pretended not to notice. He took the stranger by the arm, asked him to sit down, and inquired if she had something for them to eat. Matryona lost her temper, and said, "Yes, I do, but not for you. It seems you have drunk your brains away. You go out to buy some sheepskin and come back without even the coat you left in. What's more, you bring some half-naked tramp back with you. I don't have any supper for a pair of drunkards like you!"

Semyon replied, "That's enough of your tongue-lashing, Matryona! You might at least ask who he is." She responded, "You can at least tell me what you did with the money." Semyon dug into his pocket and took out the three-ruble note and placed it on the table. He told her that Trifonov wouldn't give him any money, but he promised it within a day or two. Matryona grew more furious. She snatched the note from the table and went to hide it. She told him: "I have no supper for you. You can't expect me to feed every naked drunkard."

Semyon asked his wife to hold her tongue and to listen to what the stranger had to say. She rambled on, "What sense will I get from a drunken fool like you? I was right in not wanting to marry an old fool like you! You sold all mother's linen for drink. And then, instead of buying sheepskins, you spend all the money on vodka." He tried hard to make his wife understand that all he had spent on vodka was a mere twenty kopecks, and he attempted to explain where he had found the stranger. She went on and on, not letting him talk, and bringing up things that had happened ten years ago.

Matryona went over and grabbed her husband's sleeve, demanding her jacket back. Semyon took off the jacket. Matryona pulled on it so hard that one sleeve came apart at the seams. She threw it over her head and walked toward the door. She stopped abruptly and decided to banish all her spiteful feelings. Her heart seemed to melt; she realized that she wanted to find out who the man really was.

Matryona observed, "If he were an honest man, he wouldn't be going around without a shirt on his back. And if you'd been doing what you were supposed to, you'd have told me where you picked up this fine young fellow!" Semyon replied, "All right, I'll tell you. I was on my way home when I saw this man sitting by the chapel, naked and frozen. Now, it's not the kind of weather to go about naked! If God must had not led me to him, he would have perished.

What could I do? Who knows what might have happened to him? So, I made him stand up, clothed him, and brought him back here. Please don't be angry, Matryona, it's sinful. Don't forget that we must all die one day."

Matryona was going to give her husband a piece of her mind again until she looked at the stranger. He sat, motionless, on the edge of the bench, hands folded on his knees, head drooping on his chest. His eyes were closed, and his face was wrinkled as though something were choking him. When Matryona said nothing, Semyon asked if there was no love of God within her. At these words, she glanced at the stranger, and her heart was filled with pity.

Matryona went to the stove, took out the supper, placed a cup on the table, and poured some kvass. Then she brought out the last slice of bread and set out a knife and some spoons. "Please eat, she said." Semyon nudged the stranger and invited him to sit at the table.

Semyon divided the bread into small pieces, and they began to eat. Matryona sat at a corner of the table, resting her head on her arm, gazing at the stranger. She was filled with pity, and her heart went out to him. Suddenly, his face brightened, the wrinkles disappeared, and he looked up at her and smiled.

After supper, Matryona asked the stranger where he was from, and again he said he was not from these parts. When she asked how he came to be by the roadside, he said he could not tell her. When she asked who had stolen his clothes, he said, "God punished me." She asked, "You were just sitting there, naked? The stranger replied: "Yes, naked and freezing. And then Semyon saw me and took pity on me. He took off his coat, put it over me, and brought me home with him. You have given me food and drink and shown compassion. God will reward you!"

Matryona picked up the old shirt of Semyon's that she had been patching and handed it to the stranger. Then she found him some trousers. She said, "I see that you have no shirt, so put this on and lie down where you like—on the sleeping bench or the bench over the stove." The stranger took off the coat, put on the shirt and trousers, and lay on the bench. Matryona blew out the candle, took the coat, and joined her husband on the bench over the stove.

Matryona pulled the coat over her and lay down. However, she did not fall asleep; she could not get the stranger out of her mind. When she remembered that he had eaten their last slice of bread, that they would have none for tomorrow, and that she had given him the shirt and trousers, she became dejected. However, when she recalled his smile, her heart leapt. She lay awake for a long time, and she noticed that Semyon was awake too.

Matryona reminded her husband that they had eaten the last slice of bread, and that she hadn't prepared any more. She thought she might be able to borrow some from a neighbor. Semyon assured her that they would get by; they wouldn't starve. Matryona observed that the stranger seemed to be a good man, although he didn't tell them anything about himself. Semyon said, "Maybe he can't." Matryona commented that they were always giving, and asked Semyon, "Why doesn't anybody ever give us anything?" Semyon didn't know how to answer that, so he just turned over and went to sleep.

When Semyon woke up the next morning, the children were still asleep and his wife had gone to a neighbor's house to borrow some bread. The stranger was sitting on the bench and looking up at him. His face was brighter than the evening before. Semyon said, "Well, my friend. The belly needs food and the body clothes. We all have to earn a living, so what sort of work can you do?" The stranger replied that he couldn't do anything.

Semyon was surprised and said that if a man has the will he can learn anything. The stranger told Semyon he was willing to work for a living. Semyon asked him what his name was, and he replied, "Mikhail." Semyon told him, "Well, Mikhail, if you don't want to tell us about yourself, that's your affair. But we have to earn our living. If you do as I tell you, I'll see that you have enough to eat." Mikhail promised to learn how to work and asked to be told what to do.

Semyon took a piece of yarn, wound it around his fingers, twisted it, and suggested that Mikhail try it. Mikhail caught on quickly and wound and twisted the yarn just as Semyon did. Semyon showed him how to wax it, and Mikhail understood at once. Then he showed him how to draw the yarn through and how to stitch. Again, the student learned quickly. Within three days, he was making shoes as though he had been making them all his life.

Mikhail worked steadily and ate very little. When a job was finished, he looked up, waiting for the next assigned task. He never left the cottage, spoke only when spoken to, and never joked or laughed. In fact, the only time they had seen him smile was the first evening, when Matryona had given him supper.

A year later, Mikhail was still living with Semyon and working for him. Word got around that Semyon's workman could make better and stronger boots than anyone else. People came from all around the district for new shoes and boots, and Semyon prospered.

One winter day, Semyon and Mikhail were sitting at their work benches when a three-horse carriage drove up to the cottage. A young boy jumped down from the coachman's seat and opened the carriage door. A gentleman in a fur coat stepped out, walked up to the front door, and climbed the steps. Matryona rushed to open the door. The gentleman had to duck his head to clear the door frame. His head almost touched the ceiling; he seemed to fill an entire corner of the room.

Semyon had never seen anyone like the gentleman. Semyon was lean, Mikhail was thin, and Matryona was skinny. This man had a full red face, a bull's neck, and a solid physique. He seemed like someone from another world. The visitor took off his coat, sat on the bench, and asked, "Who is the master bootmaker here?" Semyon acknowledged that he was.

The gentleman shouted at the boy to bring in the leather he had brought with him. The boy placed it on the table. The man asked Semyon if he knew what kind of leather it was. Semyon told him that he could tell it was of very good quality. He told Semyon that it was German and had cost twenty rubles.

The visitor asked Semyon to make a pair of boots out of it. Then he yelled at him: "Now, see you don't forget for whom you're making them and the quality of the leather you'll be using. I want a pair of boots that will last a year without losing their shape or coming apart at the stitches. If you can do the job, take the leather and cut it up. But if you can't, you'd better tell me here and now. I'm warning you: if the boots split or lose their shape before the year is out, I'll have you put in prison. But if they keep their shape and don't split for a year, I'll pay you ten rubles."

Semyon wasn't sure how to reply. He asked Mikhail, who advised him to take on the job. Semyon told the gentleman he would make the boots. The man directed the boy to take off his left boot, and told Semyon to take his measurements. The man told Semyon not to make the boots too tight in the leg.

Then the gentleman noticed Mikhail and asked who he was. Semyon told him that he was his master craftsman, and that he would be making the boots. The gentleman reminded Mikhail that the boots had to last a whole year. When Semyon turned to Mikhail, he saw that he was not even looking at the gentleman, but staring behind him into the corner, as though someone was there. Mikhail kept staring until suddenly he smiled, and his whole face lit up. The gentleman asked, "What are you grinning at, idiot? You'd better see that the boots are ready on time!" Mikhail assured him that they would be. The gentleman donned his fur coat and left in his carriage.

Semyon noted that having taken on the work, he hoped that it didn't get them in trouble. The leather was expensive and the gentleman was short-tempered, so he hoped they wouldn't fail. He told Mikhail, since his eyes were sharper than his and his hands were more skilled, to take the measurements and start cutting the leather. Semyon said that he would sew the pieces together later.

Mikhail took the leather, spread it on the table, folded it in two, and began cutting. Matryona went over to watch Mikhail working and was surprised to see what he was doing. She knew about boot-making and could see that instead of cutting the leather into the usual shape for boots, he was cutting it into round pieces. She was tempted to point it out but thought, "Maybe I don't understand how a gentleman's boots should be made. Mikhail knows best; I won't interfere."

When he had finished cutting, Mikhail started sewing the pieces—not with two ends, as he should have for boots, but with one end, as if for slippers. Although this also surprised Matryona, she did not interfere. Mikhail sewed until midday. When Semyon got up from his bench and saw that Mikhail had made a pair of slippers from the gentleman's leather, he groaned.

Semyon thought, "I don't understand how Mikhail, who's been with me for a full year without making a mistake, could make such dreadful mess of things. The gentleman ordered welted high boots, and he's made slippers without soles and ruined the leather. How can I face the gentleman? I can't replace leather of that quality."

Semyon asked Mikhail, "What have you done, my friend? The

gentleman ordered high boots and just look at what you've made." He was about to give Mikhail a stern lecture when someone knocked at the door. They looked out of the window and could see a rider tethering his horse. When the door was opened, the young boy who had accompanied the gentleman walked in. He said that he had come about the boots. When asked what he needed, he replied, "The master won't be needing them, he's dead. He died in the carriage even before we got home. When we reached the house, he was already stiff, stone-dead, and we really struggled getting him out of the carriage."

The mistress told me to come back here and said, "Tell that shoemaker that the gentleman won't be needing his boots, but instead to make a pair of soft corpse-slippers as soon as he can." She instructed me to wait until they were ready. Mikhail collected the scraps of leather from the table and rolled them up. Then he took the soft slippers he had made, wiped them with his apron, and handed them to the boy. The boy took the roll and the slippers, wished them good luck, and left.

Years passed until Mikhail was in his sixth year with Semyon. His style of living had not changed. He never went out and spoke only when spoken to. In six years, he had smiled only twice—when Matryona had first given him supper and when the rich gentleman had called. Semyon thought the world of his workman and no longer inquired where he was from. His main fear was that Mikhail would leave him.

One day, everyone was at home. Matryona was working at the oven, and the children were scampering around the room. Semyon was stitching at one window, and Mikhail was putting a heel on a boot at the other. One of the little boys looked out of the window and exclaimed, "Look, uncle Mikhail! There's a lady with two little girls. I think they are coming here. One of the girls is limping." Mikhail put his work down and looked out into the street.

Semyon was surprised. Mikhail had never looked out before, but now he was glued to the window, staring at something. Semyon saw a well-dressed woman with two little girls in fur coats coming toward the cottage. The girls were so alike, it would have been difficult to tell them apart were it not that one had a crippled left leg and walked with a limp.

The woman climbed the steps and knocked on the door. She let the girls enter first and greeted everyone when she came in. The woman sat at the table with the girls. Semyon welcomed them, and asked what they could do for them. The woman said that would like some shoes made for the girls for the spring. Semyon said that they could make them, either welted or lined with linen, although they had not made such small ones before. Semyon introduced Mikhail as his master shoemaker. Semyon turned to Mikhail, who had stopped working and had his eyes fixed on the little girls.

Semyon was astonished. True, the girls were very pretty — pleasingly plump with dark eyes and rosy cheeks. They wore fine fur coats and shawls. He couldn't understand why Mikhail was staring at them as if he knew them. Semyon discussed price with the woman, and it was agreed upon. The woman lifted the lame girl onto one knee and said, "Measure her twice and make one shoe for her lame foot and three for the sound one: they take exactly the same size because they are twins."

Semyon took the necessary measurements; he inquired about the lame leg, and asked if the girl had been born that way. The woman answered: "No, she was crushed by her mother." Matryona then asked if she were their mother. The woman said that she wasn't; in fact, she wasn't even a relative. She said that they were complete strangers to her when she adopted them and that she was very fond of them.

The woman told them the girls' story. "It all started six years ago when these little girls lost their father and mother in the same week — their father was buried on Tuesday and the mother died on Friday. My husband and I were farmworkers and our yard was adjacent to theirs. The father was a loner who worked as a woodcutter. One day they were cutting down trees, and they let one fall on him, crushing him. They had hardly got him back to the village when his soul went up to heaven.

"The same week, his widow gave birth to twins — these little girls. She was a poor woman, all on her own, with no other women to help her. Alone she gave birth, and alone she died. The next morning, I went to see how she was, but the poor thing was already stiff and cold. When she died, she rolled over onto this little girl and twisted her leg out of shape. The villagers came, washed the body, and laid it out. Then they made a coffin and buried her. They were good people.

"The two girls were left alone in the world, and who was to look after them? I was the only woman in the village who'd had a baby at the time, and I had been breast-feeding my son for eight weeks. The men of the village suggested that I take care of them for a time, while they decided what to do long-term. I was young and well-nourished and had plenty of breast milk for three babies. But it was God's will that I should nurse these little girls and bury my own child before he was two years old.

"God never gave me a second child. Subsequently, we became quite well off. My husband earns good money, and we live well. Since we have no children of our own, I'd be terribly lonely without these two little girls. How can I help but love them?"

The woman pressed the lame girl to her with one hand and wiped tears from her cheeks with the other. Matryona observed, "There's a lot of truth in the saying that we can live without a mother or a father, but we can't live without God." They chatted for a while, and the woman got up to leave. Semyon and his wife saw them out, and then they looked at Mikhail. He was sitting there with his arms folded, looking up, and smiling.

Semyon asked, "What is it?" Mikhail rose from the bench, put down his work, took off his apron, bowed to Semyon and Matryona, and said, "Please forgive me, good people. God has forgiven me, so please forgive me too." The shoemaker and his wife saw a light shining from Mikhail.

Semyon stood up, bowed in turn, and said, "I can see that you are no ordinary mortal, and I cannot detain you any longer or question you. But please tell me a few things. Why were you so miserable when I first found you and brought you home? And why, when my wife gave you supper, did you smile and from that time onwards brighten up? And why, when that rich gentlemen ordered those boots, did you smile again and become even more cheerful? And why, when that woman brought those little girls here just now, did you smile a third time and become the very picture of joy? Please tell me, Mikhail. What is that light coming from you, and why did you smile three times?"

Mikhail replied, "The light is radiating from me because I had been punished, but now God has forgiven me. And I smiled three times because I was commanded to discover three truths, and I have discovered them. I discovered the first truth when your wife took pity on me—when I smiled for the first time. The second truth I discovered when that rich gentleman ordered the boots—then I smiled again. And just now, when I saw those two little girls, I discovered the last of the three truths—and I smiled for the third time."

Semyon asked, "Tell me, Mikhail, why did God punish you, and what are the three truths, so that I may know them?"

Mikhail replied, "God punished me because I disobeyed him. Yes, I was an angel in heaven, and the Lord sent me down to earth to take a woman's soul. I flew down and saw the woman lying there. She was sick, all alone, and had just given birth to twins, two little girls. There they were, next to their mother, but she was unable to put them to her breasts.

"When she saw me, she understood that God had sent me to take her soul. She burst into tears and said, 'Angel of the Lord! My husband has just been buried, killed by a falling tree. I have no sister, no aunt, no grandmother—no one to bring up my little orphans. So please don't take my soul, let me suckle my babies, bring them up, and set them on their feet. Children cannot live without a father and a mother!'

"And I did what she asked, pressed one little girl to her breast, put the other in her arms, and ascended into heaven. I flew to God and told Him, 'I cannot bring myself to take the soul of a woman who has just borne twins. The father was killed by a falling tree, and the mother has just given birth and begged me not to take her soul.' She pleaded, 'Let me suckle my children, bring them up, and set them on their feet. Children cannot live without a father or a mother.' So I did not take that woman's soul.

"God said, 'If you go down to earth and take that woman's soul, you will discover three truths: you will learn what dwells in man, what is not given to man, and what men live by. When you have learned these truths, you shall return to heaven.' So I flew down to earth again and took the mother's soul. The babies dropped from her breasts, and her body rolled over on one of them, crushing her leg. Then I rose above the village wishing to return her soul to God; however, I was seized by a strong wind, and my wings drooped and fell off. Her soul alone returned to God, and I fell to earth by the roadside."

Semyon and Matryona now realized whom they had taken in to live with them. They wept for joy and fear. The angel said, "I was alone and naked in that field. Never before had I known the needs of man, never had I known cold or hunger. But now I was an ordinary mortal, cold, hungry, and not knowing what to do. Then I saw a chapel in the field, built for the glory of God. So I went to it to seek shelter. But it was locked, and I could not enter. So I sat down behind it to be sheltered from the wind.

"Evening came, and I was famished, freezing, and in pain. I heard a man coming down the road. He was carrying a pair of boots and talking to himself. For the first time since I had become man, I saw the mortal face of man. It terrified me, and I turned away. I could hear this man wondering how to protect his body from the winter cold and feed his wife and children. I thought, 'I am perishing with cold and hunger, but here is someone whose only thought is how to find a warm coat for himself and his wife, and food for his family. I cannot expect any help from him.'

"When the man saw me, he frowned, looked even more terrifying, and passed me by. I was desperate. But suddenly, I heard him coming back. As I looked at him, he no longer seemed the same man. Before his face had borne the stamp of death; now he had come alive again, and in that face I could see God. He came up to me, clothed me, and took me home.

"When we arrived, a woman came out to met us, and she spoke. This woman was even more terrifying than the man. Her breath seemed to come from the grave, and I was almost choked by that deathly stench. She wished to cast me out into the cold; I knew if she did that, I would die. Then her husband told her to think of God, and at once she was transformed. When she had given us supper, I returned the look she gave me and saw that death no longer dwelt in her, but life. And in her too, I could see God.

"I recalled God's first lesson: thou shalt learn what dwelleth in man. And now I knew that it is love that dwells in man. I was overjoyed that God had begun to reveal what He had promised to reveal, and I smiled for the first time. But I did not know the whole truth yet. I did not know what is not given to man, and what men live by.'

"I came to live with you, and one year passed. One day a rich gentleman came to order a pair of boots that would last a year without splitting or losing their shape. When I looked at him, I saw the Angel of Death, standing behind him. No one but I could see that angel, and I knew that he would take that gentleman's soul before sunset. And I thought, 'Here is a man who wants to provide for himself for a year from now but does not know that by evening he will be dead.' I remembered God's second lesson: thou shalt learn what is not given to man.

"What dwells in man I already knew. Now I knew that which is not given to man: It is not given to him to know his bodily needs. And I smiled a second time. I rejoiced that I had seen my fellow angel, and that God had revealed His second truth. But still I did not know everything. I did not understand what it is that men live by. And so I lived on, waiting for God to reveal this last truth to me.

"In my sixth year, the woman came here with the two little girls. I recognized the girls and learned how they had stayed alive. After this discovery, I thought, 'The mother pleaded with me for her children's sake, and I believed what she said, thinking that children cannot live without a father or a mother. But the other woman nursed them and brought them up.' And when I saw how much love this woman had for the children and how she wept over them, I saw the living God in her and understood what men live by. I realized that God had revealed His last lesson and had forgiven me. So I smiled for the third time."

The angel's body was bathed and robed in light, so that the eye could not look upon it. The angel's voice grew louder, as though it came not from him, but from heaven itself. The angel said, "I have learned that men live not by selfishness, but by love. It was not given to the mother to know what her children needed for their lives. Nor was it given for the rich man to know what his true needs were. Nor is it given for any man to know, before the sun has set, whether he will need boots for his living body or slippers for his corpse.

"When I became a mortal, I survived not by thinking of myself, but through the love that dwelt in a passer-by and his wife, and by the compassion and love they showed me. The two orphans' lives were preserved, not by what others may have intended for them, but by the love and compassion that dwelt in the heart of a woman, a complete stranger. Indeed, all men live not by what they may intend for their own well-being, but by love that dwells in others.

"Previously, I had known that God gave life to men and desired that they live. But then I came to understand something else: that

God does not wish men to live apart, and that is why He does not reveal to each man what he needs for himself alone. On the contrary, He wishes men to live in peace and harmony with each other, and for this reason He has revealed to each one of them what all men need, as well as themselves.

"I understood that men think that they live by caring only about themselves. In reality, they live by love alone. He who dwells in love dwells in God, and God in him, for God is love." The angel sang the Lord's praises, and the cottage shook with the sound of his voice. The roof parted, and a pillar of fire rose from earth to heaven. Semyon and his wife and children prostrated themselves. The angel's wings unfurled, and he soared into the sky. When Semyon came to his senses, the cottage was just as it had always been, and no one was there but him and his family.

Moral: We should live not by selfishness, but by love.

Based on: Leo Tolstoy, "What Men Live By," *How Much Land Does a Man Need? and Other Stories*

Epilogue

The ultimate value of great legends lies in their inspiring poetry,
Their moral values and their attitude to life.
It is poetically right for the blinded Samson to bring down
The pillars of the Philistine temple upon his enemies and himself,
For Robert Bruce to learn a lesson in resolution from the spider,
For Roland in his obdurate pride to sound the great horn too late
    at Rencesvals,
For the glory of Arthur and his champions of the Round Table
To end in betrayal, destruction and bitter grief.
In legend courage, loyalty, generosity, and greatness of heart
Are upheld against cowardice, treachery, meanness and
    poorness of spirit.
The lesson which the supreme heroes of legend and history have
    to teach is that life need not be petty,
That existence can be vivid, exciting, and intense,
That the limits of human reach and achievement are
Not as narrow and restricted as they so often seem.

Richard Cavendish, *Legends of the World*

Notes

Many of these legends and tales have been passed down by story-tellers and have evolved in the telling. The author gratefully acknowledges the works of other authors, including those from earlier eras, such as James Baldwin (1841-1925), Jesse Lyman Hurlbut (1843-1930), and Andrew Lang (1844-1912), who preserved our heritage and whose endeavors provided many of the stories presented here. These legends and tales have been rewritten to provide a consistent writing style.

Vector art is from IMSI's MasterClips Collection, 1895 Francisco Blvd. East, San Rafael, CA 94901-5506, USA

Bibliography

Ausubel, Nathan, ed. *A Treasury of Jewish Folklore: Stories, Traditions, Legends, Humor, Wisdom, and Folk Songs of the Jewish People*. New York: Crown, 1948.

Baldwin, James. *Favorite Tales of Long Ago*. New York: E. P. Dutton, 1955.

—. *Fifty Famous People: A Book of Short Stories*. New York: American Book, 1912.

—. *Fifty Famous Stories Retold*. New York: American Book, 1896.

—. *Thirty More Famous Stories Retold*. New York: American Book, 1905.

Barnard, Mary. *The Mythmakers*. Athens, Ohio: Ohio University Press, 1966.

Becquer, Gustavo Adolfo. *Romantic Legends of Spain*. New York: Thomas Y. Crowell, 1909.

Bennett, William, ed. *The Book of Virtues: A Treasury of Great Moral Stories*. New York: Simon & Schuster, 1993.

Bierlein, J. F. *Parallel Myths*. New York: Ballantine Books, 1994.

Calvino, Italo, ed. *Italian Folktales*. New York: Harcourt Brace Jovanovich, 1956.

Cavendish, Richard. *Legends of the World*. New York: Schocken Books, 1982.

Colum, Padraic. *Orpheus: Myths of the World*. New York: Macmillan, 1930.

Crossley-Holland, Kevin, ed. *Folk-Tales of the British Isles*. New York: Pantheon Books, 1985.

Cruse, Amy. *The Book of Myths*. New York: Gramercy Books, 1993.

Eliot, Alexander. *The Global Myths: Exploring Primitive, Pagan, Sacred, and Scientific Mythologies*. New York: Continuum, 1993.

Esenwein, J. Berg, and Marietta Stockard. *Children's Stories and How to Tell Them*. Springfield, MA: Home Correspondence School, 1919.

Goodrich, Norma Lorre. *Myths of the Hero*. New York: Orion Press, 1958.

Harrell, John and Mary, eds. *A Storyteller's Treasury*. New York:

Harcourt, 1977.

Hodgetts, Edith M. S. *Tales and Legends from the Land of the Tzar*. London: Griffith Farran, 1891.

The Holy Bible. New York: The Douay Bible House, 1945.

Hurlbut, Jesse Lyman. *Hurlbut's Story of the Bible for the Young and Old*. New York: Holt, 1957.

Irving, Washington. *The Alhambra: Tales and Sketches of the Moors and Spaniards*. New York: A. L. Burt, 1924.

Jimenez-Landi, Antonio. *The Treasure of the Muleteer and Other Spanish Tales*. Garden City: Doubleday, 1974.

Klees, Emerson. *Legends and Stories of the Finger Lakes Region*. Rochester, NY: Friends of the Finger Lakes Publishing, 1995.

—. *More Legends and Stories of the Finger Lakes Region*. Rochester, NY: Friends of the Finger Lakes Publishing, 1997.

Lee, F. H. *Folk Tales of All Nations*. New York: Tudor Publishing, 1930.

Mabie, Hamilton Wright. *Heroes Every Child Should Know*. New York: Doubleday, Page, 1906.

Rugoff, Milton, ed. *A Harvest of World Folk Tales*. New York: Viking Press, 1949.

Scott, Sir Walter. "History of Scotland." *Tales of a Grandfather*. Boston: Ticknor and Fields, 1861.

Spence, Lewis. *Legends & Romances of Spain*, London: George G. Harrap, 1920.

Tolstoy, Leo. *How Much Land Does a Man Need? and Other Stories*. New York: Penguin Books, 1993.

—. *Tales of Courage and Conflict*. Garden City, NY: Hanover House, 1958.